the Dungeon

the Dungeon

Lynne Reid Banks

我跟你到死

An imprint of HarperCollins*Publishers*

First published in Great Britain by Collins in 2002
This edition published by Collins 2003

Collins is an imprint of HarperCollins*Publishers* Ltd,
77-85 Fulham Palace Road,
Hammersmith, London W6 8JB

The HarperCollins website address is
www.**fire**and**water**.com

1 3 5 7 9 8 6 4 2

Text copyright © Lynne Reid Banks 2002

The author asserts the moral right to be
identified as the author of the work.

ISBN 0 00 713778 8

Printed and bound in Great Britain by
Clays Ltd, St Ives plc

To Chris, who read it first

Chapter One

Bruce McLennan, Scottish laird and master of all that lay in his sight, stood on the edge of a deep, wide, square pit. It was dug into the top of a crag that stood next to a river. The men who had dug it were standing around it, filthy, tired and covered with sweat. There were over a hundred of them, all tenants of the laird's, and it had taken them two months to level the hilltop and dig the pit in one corner. All the work had been done with picks and shovels, and the spoil carried away in big baskets and cast down the hill. From a distance it looked as if the hill had been decapitated, with the pale blood of the inner ground flowing down its sides.

Bruce McLennan stared down into the newly-excavated depths. At the moment there was just a hole in the ground. But he could already see a dungeon.

He could imagine it lined with big blocks of stone. He could imagine iron rings in the walls, to which prisoners could be chained. He could imagine the huge wooden door with iron panels and hinges and lock, and a heavy brass key. He could even foreshadow a man, languishing down there in the raw depths, his prisoner — helpless, wretched, defeated — chained to the wall, not just a symbol of conquest but a real man, one he hated with his whole heart. Or what was left of it, for this villain had destroyed all that was precious and love-filled in the life of McLennan, leaving him a hollow man burning for vengeance, but not headstrong enough to go after it until he was ready.

At the laird's side stood Master Douglas of Berwick. This man had led the building of fortresses and castles in several parts of Scotland, England and Wales. Only Bruce McLennan's considerable wealth had gained him the services of this master builder, who stood now at a rough table that had been set up for him. He was poring over a number of large pieces of slate, on which were scratched drawings that he and McLennan had made together. He alone knew McLennan's intentions and the extent of his ambition for this project.

'Foreman!' McLennan shouted. 'Where the devil are ye?

Och, there y'are! Now then.' He chose one of the slate-plans and put it into the work-stained hands of his main man. 'Here's how the dungeon is to look when it's finished, do ye ken?'

The foreman took the drawing and stared at it. It was a good drawing. He could feel he was looking down into the finished chamber, as if he were a bird flying above it, or rather, since of course it would have a ceiling, a spider crawling over it. A faint shudder passed across his shoulders. It would be a fearful place to be locked into.

'Aye, sir.'

'And here,' McLennan produced more slates, 'are the plans for the castle.'

The first plan showed a bird's-eye view of an imposing square structure with a courtyard, or ward, in the centre. In this was a well – a vital adjunct should the castle ever come under siege. At the corners of the ward were four round crenellated towers (the dungeon would be underneath one of them), linked by walls with battlements, a main gate with two massive U-shaped gatehouses, a small postern gate that led down to the river, and a deep-dug moat in front, to be crossed by a ramp and drawbridge.

The next plan showed a side elevation, with very narrow

windows, like slits, so arrows could fly out but couldn't so easily fly in. A third, fourth and fifth gave a lot of detail, showing many rooms: a great hall, stables, storerooms and servants' quarters, all to be built against the inside of the thick walls. The foreman stared at these in admiration. It would be an exciting and difficult project, even for an experienced engineer like himself.

It would need many workers – hundreds, possibly over a thousand. Digging was just the start of it! They would need quarriers to bring the stone for the building; stone masons to build the mighty walls, many feet thick, with skins of mortared stones packed with rubble between; blacksmiths to make and mend iron tools; plumbers to create cisterns and latrines; and carpenters to make scaffolding and later, the floors, for the castle would have two storeys. In addition there would have to be hundreds of unskilled labourers.

'Any questions?' barked his master.

'Aye, m'laird. How are the needful workers to be found? Where are they to live?'

McLennan picked up another plan from the pile of slates on the table.

'Ye see where my house is, down there below?' He pointed to a large timber-framed manor house at the foot of the crag. 'It won't stand alone for long! Men will come when they are offered good wages, cheap homes and farmland, and my protection against danger. While the first levelling and digging is going on, ye're to send men as far afield as Edinburgh to recruit. Word will spread! By the time I get back from my travels, I'll lay there'll be a small town where my house is, and farms and hamlets besides, all over my land.'

'Ye plan a journey, m'laird?'

'Aye. A long, long journey,' replied McLennan drily. He glanced at the master builder at his side. 'And that'll please you, Master Douglas, I dunna doubt! Ye'll have a free hand, without me here to nag and interfere with ye. As for you, Foreman,' he added, 'dunna think because the cat's away, the mice can play. I've engaged some overseers to make sure no one slacks.'

The foreman bit back a retort. It irked him sometimes that this man, as lowborn as himself, and lower, should have such power over him. Especially now, since he was so sorely changed from the man he had been once. Not that that was to be wondered at, after what had happened to him.

'Will ye afford a wall around this – this township, m'laird?'

McLennan thought for a moment. 'There's no need for a stone wall. A wooden palisade with earth ramparts within will suffice.'

'And if there should be a raid or any trouble while ye're away, what then?'

'We're too far from the border for the English to come at us.'

'I was thinking of a closer enemy,' the foreman said under his breath.

There was a bad moment of silence. Then McLennan said, in an unnaturally quiet voice, 'Lightning doesna strike the same place twice.'

The man had the sense to say no more on that subject. Instead he said respectfully, 'I trust ye'll no' run into danger yourself, sir.'

'I trust I will,' returned McLennan obscurely.

The foreman thought he had misheard.

'How long will ye be away, sir?'

McLennan lost patience and roared at him. 'How the blazes d'ye expect me to know that? My plan is to travel to the far ends of the earth. Whatever I find there, I'm planning to see plenty of it, before I turn around and come back!'

The foreman looked at the plans again. When his laird flew into these sudden rages, it was better not to meet his eyes.

'Sir?' he ventured timidly.

'Well?'

'I see no chapel on the plans.'

'That's because there will be none.'

Now the man's head did come up, and he looked at his master. Bruce McLennan towered over him. He had flaming red hair and a bushy red beard. His strong, bare legs below his kilt were planted apart; his arms, brawny and hairy as a pig's flanks, were folded across his chest, compressing his plaid which blew back in the wind. He looked a mighty man indeed. Not one to cross – every man present knew that.

'No – place of worship, m'laird?'

'Not in my castle. If, outside it, ye feel the need for a church, ye can build one, but in your ain time and with your ain money.'

There was a tense silence. Was there a touch of blasphemy here? Many eyes went to Master Douglas, who was reputed to be a devout Christian; but if he had felt scandalised on first learning of this unheard-of omission, he showed nothing now.

'How long have we to complete the work?'

'Here is the only answer I'll give ye,' said the master. 'When I choose to come back, my castle had better be standing up against yon sky, and my dungeon had better be below it. If not, I'll hang the lot o' ye from whatever ye *have* built. Do I make myself understood?'

There was a cowed silence around the dungeon pit. There was hostility in that silence, too, but it was lost on their master. Though once he had been different, now he cared nothing for their good opinion so long as they obeyed him. And obey him they must, for he was their liege-laird, and they his tenant-serfs, not much better than slaves.

*

Half an hour after the last workman had left the site, and McLennan had retired to his house to prepare for his journey, a young boy called Finlay McLean climbed up the disturbed and treacherous slope. The sun had set beyond the river and the lad had to grope his way forward and upward over the shifting ground in deepening twilight. Several times he lost his footing and slipped and slithered down several feet, and once he fell forward on his belly and had to dig his fingers into the loose soil and stones to stop himself sliding to the bottom of the crag.

Once he had gained the levelled top, he doubled up and ran to the edge of the dungeon pit. He feared the master might be watching from his window at the foot of the hill and see his silhouette. But when he reached the pit's edge he knew he would be hidden from below, and he straightened up and stared downward into the darkening depths.

He couldn't rightly see through the shadows to the bottom. He thought he might as well be looking down into The Pit as described by the priest in the course of his many warning sermons. Fin fancied if he stumbled over the edge, he would fall and go on falling till he reached that furiously burning region in the middle of the earth, where the damned were subject to unending torment.

Yet the curiosity that had brought him up here, held him.

He knew who this dungeon had been dug for. His name was Archibald McInnes, a name Fin had never heard spoken aloud, even by his father in his own home — a farmhouse two miles away — from where he came to work in the master's stables. In whispers they spoke that name, and that name's crimes, crimes that had changed a good man, a good laird, into one to be feared. The whispers told how the whole feud had begun, with a dispute over the border between the lands of the two lairds who were neighbours. How there had been a skirmish in which the neighbour's nephew had been killed. And what followed, a tale too terrible to be told before a child; but Fin had heard it anyway, as children do who have their ears open on the brink of sleep when adults think they are over that brink, and speak more freely than they should.

A terrible tale. A dreadful happening, dark with blood and cruelty, a crime crying out for vengeance. Yes, thought Fin, shivering as he peered into the blackening depths as the sky darkened over him. If his master captured McInnes and brought him back here – as clearly he meant to, one day, when his castle was built and he had enough men owing him allegiance to be sure of success – the villain would deserve to be hurled down there, down, down, into the pitchy gloom, however deep it went, and never to be seen on the warm bright surface-earth again.

*

Fin was in the stables of the manor house a week later, on the day Bruce McLennan set off on his travels. He had not had the honour of grooming and saddling his horse. Robert the head groom did that. Nor was it Fin who led the animal out and handed the reins to the master. But it was Fin's job to hold the opposing stirrup as the laird mounted. He had almost to swing on it to balance the master's weight and keep the saddle from slipping.

McLennan didn't notice the young tow-headed lad level

with his heel as he swung himself into the saddle. He couldn't know, as he scraped the boy's knuckles with his boot, what a fateful role this grubby nondescript boy, staring up at him in awe, would play in his future. He left him behind as he left everything behind, and rode away without a glance back.

*

He'd had no one to say goodbye to. He had handed the keys of his house to Master Douglas. It was full of appalling memories and he was glad to be shot of it for ever. He wouldn't need it when he came back. He'd have a castle to live in by then – a castle with a dungeon. The idea of it was like balm spread over a wound, in a place in his soul even deeper than the dungeon pit.

'Do unto others!' he thought fiercely as he rode. So said the scriptures. Aye. Do unto others as they have done unto you.

*

He rode down the length of the northern island that comprises Scotland, England and Wales, to its south coast. This took days – and several horses, for he was a hard rider. He put up at wayside inns when he found them, and when he didn't he would camp outdoors. When there was a reasonable road (the best had been built by the Romans ten centuries before) and some moonlight, he would ride far into the night to put off having to sleep alone under the sky, or eat and drink without company to distract his mind.

Sometimes when he was sitting by a campfire on some desolate moor or under some ancient oak in the depths of a forest, memories would come back to him of his childhood in a modest croft on the island where his father was a fisherman and his mother spun sheep's wool and wove cloth from it to sell. He remembered these two people he had loved, and his brothers and sister, and the happiness he had known as a wild young boy, torn between family affection and a driving restlessness. Sometimes he even thought he could smell the good smells of fish and the sea, of the steaming soap-vats in which his mother washed the wool; he would hear the sounds of young lambs in the spring bleating for the ewes, and feel the warmth of his bed with his brothers sleeping close to him while the peat fire made a glow on the low, whitewashed ceiling until it died away.

These pleasant memories had a double power. They let him relive his happy, humble childhood, and they made him proud, by contrast, of his present high position. It was not often a fisherman's son rose to become a laird, owner of a large estate with command over several hundred tenant-serfs who owed him unquestioning loyalty. And he had earned this elevation, not merely inherited it.

He might have blushed to remember why he had resisted becoming a fisherman like his father – seasickness – but he had forgotten that. What he remembered was travelling south alone to volunteer in the King's service against the English, who were striving fruitlessly but bloodily to subdue Scotland. He did the King great service, even saving his life on one occasion when he was thrown from his horse on the field of battle. What a piece of miraculous good fortune that the young McLennan had been nearby at that fateful moment. Nineteen years old, strong and quick and with the recklessness of a highland bull, McLennan had fought his way swiftly to his monarch's side, and carried him over his broad shoulder to safety while the horses trampled and neighed and the swords clashed around him... For this action, the King had rewarded him royally with land and gold, and put him in the way of a beautiful highborn wife.

But when his proud recollections reached this point, McLennan seized hold of them and slammed a door on them, a door as thick and ironbound as the one he had ordered for his dungeon.

*

At last he reached the south coast. He wandered from port to port in growing impatience, haunting the quayside taverns, hungrily watching and listening. But he could only hear of ships sailing to ports in Europe. They were not what he wanted.

Then his luck changed. He had drifted up to the Port of London. Most men from the north who had never before seen the biggest town in the islands would have spent hours and days exploring the bustling streets, some grand, some vice-ridden and squalid, yet offering much entertainment... But McLennan was single-minded. He made straight for the dockside and there, in a cheerful tavern reeking of stale ale and unwashed bodies, he met a common sailor who had heard the stories he himself had heard.

'Ho, yus, Marco-Polo-land! Chi-na, they call it. It's a rare place, they say! But you can't sail all the way there,' he went on, when McLennan had stood him some ale. 'You'd have to do as he did, the Venetian, sail to St. Jean d'Acre, the port of the Crusaders in the Holy Land, or to Constantinople – that's in Turk-land, I been there! – and after that you must go by land. A year's journey, they say, or more if the weather's against you, along the road the silk comes by.'

Chapter One

'Silk? What's that?'

'Wot, ain't you heard of silk? I ain't never seen it, but they say it's the most wonderfullest stuff in the world,' the sailor said.

'Is it food?' asked McLennan.

The man blew his ale out in a spray of laughter. 'Course not, it's not for eatin'! It's for wearin'! But you'll never feel the touch of it on your back. How they make it's a secret — it's not something that grows from the ground. I heard a venomous spider spins it, and only them that's immune to its poison can harvest it. It's that rare and costly, only royalty, or highborn lords and ladies, can buy it! It has to be brought a journey of ten thousand miles, they say, across land where no civilised man can live, for it's all desert and icy mountains, and the way plagued by tribes of the fiercest riders and fighters in the world.' He lowered his voice and put his mouth close to McLennan's ear. 'Ain't you never heard of the Mongols and Tartars?'

McLennan shook his head. His heart was beating with excitement. This was what he had dreamed of. A dangerous venture that would shut out the past and truly test his mettle!

'They're the most monstrous cruel men God ever made,' the man continued in a whisper, as if a Mongol horde might even now ride into this dingy tavern and slaughter the drinkers. 'They've conquered all the lands of the east! Chi-na, too. They rule it now, and the Chi-na men can like it or lump it. 'Tis said they've the best army since the days of Rome. Nay, better! They fight on horseback, and each man rides as if him and his horse were one beast. As to their natures—' he grimaced. '*Say no more!* If a town resists 'em, they wipe it out, down to the last man, woman and child!' And he made a throat-cutting gesture, accompanied by a graphic squelching sound. 'And that's their best weapon, for after a few massacres of that sort, none dare stand against them, so they're unbeatable!'

McLennan closed his eyes suddenly. Throat-cutting was a horror very fresh in his memory. But he set his teeth and opened his eyes again, speaking more sharply than he had meant. 'How can I get to the Turk city you named?'

'Plenty of ships going there, it's one of the great ports for the spice and gem trade,' said the sailor. 'See that captain over there? His ship's bound for the Mediterranean on tomorrow's tide. If you've money enough, go ask him if you can be his passenger.'

Chapter One

McLennan was canny. He didn't want to pay too much. He waited till the captain of the ship bound for Constantinople was reeling drunk to approach him and strike his bargain.

*

The voyage was long and dangerous, but McLennan didn't mind danger. He liked it. He'd lived with danger all his life, and he never felt fully alive if he was completely safe. Besides, the thrill of fear drove out thoughts.

What he didn't like was rough seas. In the Bay of Biscay, off the coast of Portugal, there were violent storms that threw the ship about like a cork; its crew had to struggle against wind and waves, holding on to lifelines on deck, and lashing themselves to the yards, and even so, two were swept overboard. Passengers were ordered to keep below decks.

At first this infuriated McLennan, but he was soon forced to remember he was a bad sailor. It humiliated him to be brought low with seasickness. After bouts of vomiting he would lie groaning on his hard bunk, cursing this half-forgotten weakness.

But when the sea wasn't rough, he spent a lot of time standing at the ship's rail, dreaming of the foreign land which was the goal of his journey.

How, in his distant Scottish home, had he heard of this exotic place? Some time ago a wandering pedlar had called on McLennan. He had but one arm, and the smell on him of foreign parts, and while he showed his wares, he hinted he'd been to sea as a pirate, and dropped more hints of fabulous tales he could tell.

McLennan, not usually welcoming to strangers, paid the man to spend a few days with him, so that he could listen to his traveller's tales, and his imagination had been inflamed by the sheer strangeness of what the pedlar described. Venturing to a place so outlandish would be like escaping his own world into another: a country on the other side of the world that was said to be more advanced than any nation in Europe, where lords — the equivalent in rank of McLennan — lived in incredible splendour, with scores of wives and servants, surrounded by priceless objects of unearthly beauty; where they spoke an indecipherable language, and wrote it in pictures; where the men had hair to their waists, and the women tiny feet no longer than a man's finger, and where food never sampled in the west was eaten from dishes so fine you could see the light through them.

Of course everything the pedlar told him might be lies...

But McLennan was determined not to die without seeing this place of wonders, if it truly existed.

*

The ship docked at last in Constantinople and McLennan disembarked, glad to feel the solid ground under his feet. Had he been less obsessed with the faraway country of his dreams, he would have lingered longer to explore the great Mohammedan mosques and magnificent palaces, roofed in gold and walled with beautiful painted tiles, and the crowded markets full of strange smells and stranger goods. But he'd heard the journey would take a year and cover ten thousand miles – and so there was no time to delay.

He soon learned there were inns called caravanserai where the traders gathered with their trade-goods so that they might travel together in greater safety. No one took this route alone. Here McLennan for the first time encountered the weird beast of burden called a *gamal,* bearing no more resemblance to a horse than that it had four legs and hair on its misshapen body. It was immensely tall with a hillock of flesh on its back, and its legs ended in big flat pads. It had foul breath and a temper worse than McLennan's own, but it seemed that without these creatures no one could travel or transport goods over the terrain they had to cross.

So McLennan hired one, and took the advice of its owner – given during a visit to the market, in sign language – as to his likely needs on the journey ahead. He secretly hoped he would never be called upon to mount a *gamal*, as its height above ground, and its inhospitable hump, would surely make him as seasick as clinging to the poop deck of a ship on high seas.

*

Once again McLennan's patience was tested. It took weeks for the caravan to assemble. But at last the party, consisting of about thirty men and as many *gamal* (or camels, as McLennan came to call them since he couldn't pronounce the guttural language of his servant-guide) set off, the camels heavily loaded, the men on foot.

McLennan was lucky. There was a Portuguese trader among the men, a seasoned traveller called Afonso, who had made this journey once before and who spoke a little English. At first they could hardly understand each other, but Afonso was a talkative man; before a month of the journey had passed, they could converse, and better and better as the long days and longer nights passed.

The Portuguese spoke a great deal about his wife and children and to this McLennan deafened himself. He would sit by the campfire at night and stare into it and say nothing, trying not to listen, not to remember.

'You have wife? Childs?' Afonso kept asking.

McLennan clenched his teeth and made no answer.

'You no find wife in Chi-na! No see womans there. Mans hide womans.'

'Tell me about Chi-na, never mind the "womans",' McLennan growled.

He learned much about their destination, which the Chi-na men called the Middle Kingdom, thinking it the centre of the world. From this translation of its name came the nickname some travellers gave to its inhabitants – 'Mi-Ki'.

'Those Mi-Ki no like stranger,' Afonso said. 'Trader not all time behave well. Some cheat, some steal. Get drunk. Very bad. Now Mi-Ki think all mans from west bad. They call us devils from far—'

'Foreign devils?'

'*Si*. So best is, keep quiet, no drink, do trade, go home.'

'I intend to stay,' said McLennan. But Afonso didn't believe him.

'No one stay,' he said.

'Marco Polo did,' thought McLennan. But he didn't say it aloud. It might be just a rumour that the Venetian had become a member of some kingly court and stayed many years.

Another time, when McLennan had been regaling Afonso, as they trudged along the weary miles, with tales of his prowess in battle back in Scotland, the Portuguese gave him a sideways grin. 'You like to fight?'

'I like it well enough when I choose,' McLennan answered.

'Mi-Ki rule now by Mongol king call Kublai Khan. Most great ruler in all world.'

'Aye, so I've heard.'

'You like to fight Mongol? Then you show you great warrior!'

But McLennan knew when he was being mocked. He already understood that no one could beat the Mongols.

Nevertheless, through the hard journey across the wild desert regions of central Asia, McLennan began to dream of war and battle. Action. Action was what he had always needed and craved, ever since a night when he was held immobile, bound to a door that he had all but torn from its hinges in his frenzy.

Chapter Two

The journey took many months. And if it wasn't ten thousand miles, often during the long months of travel it seemed like it. By the time they at last crossed the western borders of Chi-na, the Scotsman had to admit that his strength and endurance had been tested to their limits.

As they travelled on through the endless scattered farmlands of the north, McLennan saw little wealth and splendour, but much poverty and hard struggle for survival. The peasants of this vast land tilled it in the sweat of their faces, even more than his own serfs, though he was surprised to see that in certain ways their farming methods were better. Their fields were carved somehow into small, flat, irregular steps that followed the curve of the hills, to make the most of the land.

The peasants mainly kept their distance, except for a few that approached them to sell food, or to trade (these received short shrift from the cameleers, who had bigger game afoot in the cities). But McLennan saw enough of them to be amazed. He himself came from a mongrel race, descended from Picts, Britons, Vikings, Norman French and, far back, there was Roman blood. Some Scots were dark, some blond, some red-headed like him. They were of many shapes and sizes and casts of feature. All *these*, he thought at first, might have sprung from one egg – the travellers all had straight black hair, sallow skin, and eyes seemingly cut in half by their eyelids.

During the long journey, the travellers had eaten poorly, mainly meat and milk from the herds of the nomads they traded with in passing. But McLennan bore the simple diet stoically, feeding in his imagination on Afonso's descriptions of the food in Chi-na, which he insisted was exotic, varied and delicious. And here – in primitive inns along the caravan's route, where in the evenings they slumped exhausted with growling stomachs – here it was!

McLennan had never tasted such stuff. Little white grains was the bulk of it, with a few chopped vegetables half raw, some salt fish, some pig-meat, and occasional sauces that burned his tongue... He longed for a plate of porridge with honey and cream, some thick barley broth with chunks of fat mutton, good roast venison or beef in rich brown gravy, with bannock – real Scottish bread – to sop it up with.

Afonso mocked him. 'You say you stay here? If Mongol no kill you first, you die of empty belly! You eat Mi-Ki food, my friend – is good!' And he brought his bowl to his mouth and shovelled the stuff into it with two sticks, as the locals did. McLennan used his *dhu* – the short knife he carried in the top of his hose – to whittle a spoon, for which he was heartily laughed at.

How could he enjoy a place when he had no good meals to look forward to, and when his stomach was always either craving food or rejecting it? McLennan fell into a vile temper. He decided he hated this place. All these months of hard travelling to find a poor land full of peasants who ate disgusting things in a most idiotic manner! He kept his eyes on the ground and trudged on with the caravan, sullen, hungry and disappointed. Afonso tried to cheer him up, and when he failed, moved away and walked among the other men.

*

At last they reached their destination. As the caravan drew to a halt, amid the noise and bustle of a busy marketplace, McLennan had no choice but to look about him. And his senses reeled. He saw so many new things at once that he couldn't take them in. Crowds, colours, scents, strange structures seemed to whirl around him.

They were outside the gates of a city. There were walls – high, strong walls – and an open gate. But he didn't look through it at first. He looked at things nearest. There were tents both drab and brilliant, and stalls, and cartloads of exotic goods set out; there were merchants of several races, shouting, waving their arms, showing their wares – trading. There were many caravans of camels, donkeys, horses, mules and the strange creatures he had seen on the high plains called yaks. There were the clamouring noises and smells of all these. But most of all, there were colours.

McLennan's own world was full of drab greys, blacks, browns, duns... the purple of heather in flower and the blue of summer skies reflected in lakes were almost the brightest colours his eyes were used to. Now he thought of rainbows, jewels, paintings, flowers, the brilliant tiled alcoves of the Mohammedans... Still he could think of nothing to compare with what he could see here on every side. The

Mi-Ki merchants were holding these colours as if they had control of the waves of some multi-hued ocean, swirling them, displaying them — shimmering banners and bales and curtains of some wondrous fabric.

He moved forward, irresistibly drawn, and tried to touch one of the miraculous sheets. It looked like spun gold. He felt his bad mood suddenly lift like a rising pulse of music, and his desire to venture and to explore returned to him in a surge. His hands reached out... The merchant let him touch, just touch with the tips of his fingers. Then he snatched it away — like gossamer it floated on the air, tantalisingly out of reach, a glittering gold membrane that flashed in the sun.

Filled with excitement and eagerness, McLennan sought out Afonso, who was already deep in bargaining with a pigtailed merchant whose cart was laden with colourful bales of the shimmering cloth.

'Here's where I leave ye, my friend!' he said exuberantly. 'Thanks for your company.'

'Where you go, Scotlander? Stay close. Caravan not wait. Soon, we turn and go back. We sell our goods, then buy what we want — tea, porcelain, teak, perfume, spice, bamboo!' All these he said in the Portuguese tongue. The new words rolled themselves round McLennan's head like an incantation, but one vital word Afonso knew in English.

'Look! Silk!' The very word was like a sigh of ecstasy. He spread a thin tissue of forest green with a golden band over his arm. 'No hands!' he said, scowling with mock fierceness at the Scot's rough fingers.

McLennan had hardly touched the fabled silk and already he felt its magic. It was what he had travelled for – it stood for the allure of this new country. He was not going home yet!

'Dunna wait for me,' said McLennan. 'I'll no' be returning yet awhile.'

Afonso stared at him in bewilderment.

McLennan unloaded from his camel the woollen sack that contained his few possessions. The Portuguese saw his mind was made up.

'You will die,' he said with a shrug. But he embraced him. 'Go well. Good luck, my foolish friend. Sometimes in Lisboa I think of you. We no meet again.'

*

McLennan shouldered his bag and set off, through the great gates into the city. It was a city as different from London as a glittering comet crossing the sky is from the muddy River Thames crawling below.

It was built on a grid pattern. Roads led away in

dead straight lines, with much traffic: men on horseback, horse-drawn chariots, people-carriers on two wheels pulled by men at a brisk pace. And hundreds of men on foot. The buildings were low, but well constructed, with beautiful green-tiled roofs that curved upward at the corners (like the shoes of the Turks!) and were richly decorated with painted carvings. Steps led up to raised platforms in front of the houses and of the eating places, where McLennan could see that much of the furniture – tables, chairs, lamps, vases, pictures – was of an extraordinary delicacy, made with a skill in craftsmanship that he had never seen before.

He glimpsed gardens, half-hidden among the buildings. Not plain earthy plots for growing vegetables and fruit, but beautiful areas created for leisure. There was a curious refinement about everything, even the people.

Here were city folk, so wondrous-strange they might have dropped from the skies indeed. They wore long colourful robes and round-toed, thick-soled footwear. Their long black hair was piled on their heads, and some wore elaborate headdresses. Their wide sleeves, in which they tucked their hands, looked as if they were covered with flowers; they walked with small, elegant steps, seeming to glide along like wheeled toys. All were men.

Out of nothing more than curiosity, he looked for the women. The ones he had seen in the fields did not have small feet, but he thought, 'In the city, they're more refined – perhaps here they grow the small-boned ones.' However, no women were to be seen. McLennan was disappointed. He wanted to see how anyone could walk on feet the size of pears. But perhaps it was only a tale.

Away from the marketplace, he soon discovered that he did, indeed, strike fear and disgust, and perhaps even anger, into the hearts of these strange people, just as Afonso had said.

The children fled at the sight of him. Talk died at his approach, and men drew back from him, their faces blank but their eyes growing narrower still. He walked on, counting on his size and foreignness to protect him, doing nothing to arouse them against him.

He walked a long way, staring around him at the beautiful buildings and other fascinatingly unfamiliar sights. Suddenly he saw a group of men. They appeared to be marching; they wore something like a uniform – a sort of leather armour, headdresses that combined a head-wrapping and a pointed metal helmet, and swords worn stuck in their belts. These must surely be guards, or soldiers.

He decided to follow them. Not too close! They began to glance uneasily over their shoulders and walk faster and faster. He quickened his own pace. Before long they broke ranks and ran pell-mell. McLennan burst out laughing at the sight, and ran after them, shouting, 'Wait for me! I'll join ye!' They ran far ahead and eventually scattered, and he lost them amid the low buildings.

One of them had drawn and then dropped his weapon. It was a sword, curved, with a square-ended blade and a heavy bronze handle, thickly embossed to give a good grip. McLennan picked it up and hefted it in his hand. He liked the feel of it, and it had a keen edge. He threw it in the air several times and caught it deftly, aware that he was being watched. He ignored this and walked on, swishing the curved sword, making patterns in the air.

Suddenly – in the space of a moment – he found himself surrounded. The soldiers (if that's what they were) had regrouped and were on all sides of him, threatening him. Their swords, like the one he held, were drawn, and pointing at him.

One man stepped forward, empty-handed. He stood in front of the big Scot and began to harangue him in the strange tongue. McLennan liked his courage. Besides, he quickly saw that he was outmanoeuvred and would have to yield, so he decided to do it with good grace.

He turned the sword till he held it by the blade, bent his left arm, and offered the handle to the man across his sleeve with a courteous bow and a smile.

'Take what's yours, my manny,' he said. 'I'll no' want to be fighting the lot of ye.'

The swordless man was taken aback. But when McLennan continued to offer him his sword, he reached out from as far away as he could and snatched it. As he drew it quickly across McLennan's arm, the sharp blade sliced through his sleeve and cut his skin.

There was a gasp from the men standing menacing McLennan. Clearly they thought the sight of his own blood would send him into a rage. But McLennan merely laughed and parted the cloth to expose the wound.

'First blood to you!' he said. 'Come, let's be friends!' And he smeared some blood on his right hand, to show his wound was nothing, and offered it to the other man.

They stiffened, crouched, held their swords at the ready. But the man he faced relaxed a little, and a faint smile crossed his face. It was probably mere nervousness, but McLennan, himself smiling as broadly as he could through his red whiskers, boomed, 'So, smiling is something we share! Let's see what else we have in common.'

He dropped his bundle and held up both hands to show he was unarmed. Then he gestured to his mouth as a sign he wanted to eat and drink. He folded his arms across his tattered plaid and waited.

After exchanging talk in undertones, they formed up again and marched away from him. He followed, marching in step with them.

Chapter Three

He attached himself to the troop of armoured men.

At first they were very suspicious, even afraid of him, and despite his gold, they tried many tricks to shake him off, but he would not be shaken. They *were* soldiers, as he soon discovered when they joined with others, who had left the city in marching order under an officer and, eventually, after some days of travel away from the city, they fought their first battle.

By this time McLennan had realised these were not the dreaded Mongols with their horseback charges and unbeatable tactics; nor were they a regular army, fighting the invaders. They were a rough sort of private troop belonging to some warlord, fighting random skirmishes against others of the same kind.

These people mostly fought hand-to-hand with spears and swords, using tactics to surprise the enemy. At first McLennan fought the way he always had. When the officer gave the signal, he would throw up his kilt to show he wore nothing under it and was completely unafraid, and charge towards the enemy uttering blood-curdling war cries. His main weapon was a heavy club which he swung around his head in circles as he ran. His comrades were, at first, more startled and shocked than the enemy. But after a couple of these forays, they began to see the use of him.

When the opposing soldiers saw this foreign giant with his fiery hair and beard, running at them showing his nakedness and screaming in a foreign tongue, they often turned and fled. If he caught up with them, they wished they had run away faster. This delighted McLennan, who would rejoin his new companions roaring with laughter, even when he was covered with blood, some of which was his own.

His fellow soldiers began to take care of him. They taught him some of their language, gave him the best sleeping places and the best food – such as it was.

In general, he relished the fighting, and didn't mind the rough life; it suited him quite well. But he disliked being on a level with the other men, whom he felt himself far above, and never got used to the food, which, when the sauces were too full of the tongue-burn, made him ill. The only thing he liked to swallow – and which calmed his indigestion – was a hot brown drink made of small, dried-up green leaves. It didn't compare to rye whiskey, mead or ale, but it cheered him and put warmth into his belly. This, he learned, was the 'tea' Afonso had mentioned. To his surprise, McLennan became quite addicted to it.

All the time, he kept his eyes open for new things – new ideas. These Mi-Kis had some very clever devices with which to attack forts or, on one occasion, a walled town. One was a construction of timber, bamboo and twisted rope, on wheels so it could be moved, which could hurl enormous stones against walls or even over them with tremendous force. McLennan had heard of clumsy, hard-to-move siege-engines, with unpronounceable French names, that threw rocks or even fireballs, but he had never actually seen one. He called this Mi-Ki machine a catapult-on-wheels and made a detailed sketch of it.

*

One day, in a lull in the fighting, McLennan and his comrades were in a town belonging to their particular warlord, where they were part of the garrison, and they visited a poor teahouse. It had a straw roof and an earth floor, but unlike many such places, it had tables and stools. McLennan stamped up the wooden steps and sat down.

The owner, a woman, ran and hid behind the kitchen screen, but the other soldiers shouted after her, 'He's all right! The foreign giant is with us!' So she emerged and edged up to him cautiously.

'Give me tea,' McLennan said in his new language, and slapped the tabletop.

The woman went behind the screen. After a short time, a little girl came out with tea in a clay teapot as big as her head, and the usual unglazed cup with no handle. She walked to his table with a strange, hobbling gait and put them in front of him. She was trembling.

'Pour!' he said gruffly.

He glanced up at her under his eyebrows. She was only six or seven years old and he could see she was very frightened of him, but she did as she was told and didn't run away, or flinch at his growl. McLennan swigged back the tea. It was very good tea indeed. He said, 'More!' She poured again, her thin, fragile arms trembling with the weight of the big teapot. The other men were watching. An idea – no, an impulse – was forming in McLennan's mind. He looked at the child and saw that she was sturdy despite her small size, brave in her fear, and very obedient.

'Fetch your mother,' he grunted.

The little girl shuffled behind the screen, and soon the woman came out.

'How many daughters you have?' he said in the foreign tongue.

She seemed to have to count them. At last she held up nine fingers.

'Sell me one,' said McLennan.

The soldiers whispered in surprise. The woman stared at him as if she couldn't take it in. 'Which one do you want?'

'That one,' he said, pointing to the little girl who was peeping from behind the screen.

'No,' said the woman firmly. 'Not that one.'

McLennan felt balked. He already knew that in poorer parts of this country the selling of daughters by poor families or widows was a common way to fight starvation – he had been offered girl-children before by wretched parents who detained him with desperate cries of 'Good slave! Work hard!' about children younger than this one.

He half-glanced at the other men for guidance. Kai-fung,

the closest he had to a friend among them – the one whose sword he had picked up, that first day – was grinning knowingly.

'You want a servant? Pick another,' he said. 'For that one, she'll want too much.' He eked out his words with signs till McLennan understood.

The woman was clearly agitated. She went to the screen, pushed the little one out of sight and dragged out two or three more. They were older, and had stolid looks that promised stamina and cow-like obedience, but somehow McLennan didn't even want to glance at them. What was special about the little one? Denied her, his impulse hardened into determination.

He brought out a packet of the strange paper money they used here, which he had been using for small purchases. The woman shook her head. Reluctantly, he fished out a gold half-sovereign.

When the widow saw the gleam of gold in the man's big hand, her need overcame her reluctance. With tears in her eyes, she shooed the bigger girls out of sight and led the youngest out. Now the men laughed. They seldom laughed, and McLennan at once suspected he was being made a fool of.

'Why laugh?' he asked angrily.

They exchanged looks. Then Kai-fung pointed to her feet.

Until that moment, McLennan had never satisfied his wish to see a woman with small feet. He had almost forgotten the tales he had heard. But now he saw something that made him start upright, staring down.

Because she was still small, the smallness of her feet was not very noticeable, but still he could see that there was something peculiar about them. They looked not only smaller than one would expect, but strangely shaped.

He scowled down at them for a long time. The teahouse fell silent. The widow stood tensed, torn between desperate need for the gold and agonised reluctance to part with her youngest child. McLennan was thinking. He wanted her for a servant. She would accompany him wherever he went. If she was of the small-foot breed, why did she walk badly?

He glanced at Kai-fung. He nodded. *Buy her, she is worth it.* He knew something McLennan did not.

He looked at the child. She was tiny – doll-like, in her drab trousers and padded jacket frog-buttoned down one side. She had the usual straight black hair, cut across her brow and tied back, a round face, a mouth like a squashed berry. Her almond-shaped eyes were lowered. There was nothing, absolutely nothing about her that set

Chapter Three

her apart from thousands of other poor little Mi-Ki girls.

Yet, as he stared at her, trying to decide, she dared a glance up at him. There was a flashing moment when their eyes met. There was something – something that reminded him – but no. That was unthinkable. It must be something else that drew him. In any case, this was not a look that claimed kinship, but like that of a little animal in a trap.

In a second, without any more thought, his mind was made up. He straightened, slapped the gold coin on the table, and took the child by the arm. Some days before, he had pulled a water lily out of a pond in an idle moment to see how it grew. Her wrist felt like its stem. He led her out of the teahouse.

She had no time to say goodbye. She took nothing – almost nothing. At the last moment, one of her sisters, tears streaming down her face, rushed out from behind the kitchen screen and thrust into a fold in the child's jacket – a pathetic parting gift – a pair of eating sticks. That apart, all the little girl carried with her were her mother's last words, whispered to her as she almost pushed her on her way – pushed her lest she clutch her back.

'Remember who you are.'

Whatever she had been before, now she was Bruce McLennan's tea-slave.

Chapter Four

The child's name was Mudan, which, translated, is Peony, the name of a flower. But McLennan never knew this. He didn't need a name for her. He called her 'You' or 'Girl', in English or the new tongue. She had to hold tightly to her name in her memory or she would have forgotten it – forgotten who she was.

'*Wo shi mudan* – I am Peony,' she said solemnly over and over again in her head like a mantra – a sacred, continual prayer to the Buddha.

To be snatched from her life so suddenly was a shock. But she had been brought up to the understanding that as a girl-child, she was destined to be some man's possession. She hadn't expected it to happen yet – that was all. Nor, of course, had she ever dreamed she would become the common chattel of a foreign giant, and be taken away into a man's world of roughness and war. It was very frightening, and for the first hours, her mind was a blank, except for the repetition of her name.

*

That night, when the soldiers were in their billet, McLennan threw some straw on to the floor beside his own pallet-bed and pointed to it. Peony, worn out, lay down on it obediently, drawing her knees up to her chest for warmth. Her feet again caught the Scotsman's attention. The toes seemed to come to a point under her cloth shoes and the insteps were high — they really did look like pears. He beckoned to Kai-fung.

'Why feet thus?' he asked stiltedly, using the new words.

'They are bound.'

'What's that?'

The other man knelt down and took the child's cloth shoes off. McLennan saw her shrink and wince.

Under the shoes were strips of dirty cloth that wrapped each foot. They were tied very tight. McLennan scowled. 'Who do this — her mother?' Kai-fung nodded. 'But why?'

With signs and simple words, Kai-fung tried to explain. The feet of some girls were bound tight to keep them small, to stop their growth. This made the girls, when they grew up, more desirable to men.

At last, McLennan understood, or rather, guessed. The woman in the teahouse, having many daughters, had bound the feet of the youngest in the hope that she would be worth a high bride price when she grew up.

He stared down at this deformed creature he had paid a gold coin for and felt anger burn inside him. He would not allow himself to feel pity for her – or to feel anything for her. She was spoiled goods. The mother, who had kept her other daughters natural and uncrippled so they could work, had sold him one that was only meant for decoration – who would be lame and good for nothing.

'I don't want her!' he shouted suddenly.

'You can't take her back.'

'She's no good like this!'

'In a few years you can marry her.'

'What? WHAT?' roared McLennan in a fury.

Kai-fung, seeing he had given offence, was silent.

'Take them off,' McLennan said. 'Take those rags off her feet! Maybe they'll grow if you unbind her!' He said most of it in English. Kai-fung shook his head, stood up and went back to his pallet.

'Then I will!' roared McLennan.

He knelt down and started to unfasten the bandages.

The child curled up and began to utter sharp yelps of pain. McLennan ignored this. He was not gentle. He almost tore off the bindings that had made his bargain so bitter. But when he got the first foot free of them, he stopped cold, and his stomach turned over. He barely stumbled outside the billet before he vomited. Then, very slowly, he came back and continued. Hard as he was, and used to terrible sights, those little, tortured feet somehow froze his anger, though what replaced it in his heart would be hard to describe, for normal pity had been crushed there. He only knew it sickened him.

When he had bared her feet and made himself look at them, he spoke directly to her for the first time.

'Ye'll no' be wearing those rags,' he said. 'Your feet must heal and grow and that's all about it.'

Of course she understood not a word of this. McLennan went on staring at her feet, curled under, the toes beginning to sink into the soles. They stank like something rotten. No wonder she had given him that look of something wounded and in a trap. Her own mother—! It had crossed his mind, seeing the beautiful things these people made, that they might be more scientific and civilised than his own, but now he changed his mind. He wondered if it was too late for the feet to right themselves, or if he had better not simply cut his losses and leave her here.

Half a sovereign! No. She belonged to him now.

He called the billet-woman who had brought them food earlier. He gave her paper money to wash Peony's feet, rub them with ointment and wrap them loosely in clean strips.

He couldn't sleep that night for the child sobbing in agony as the blood in the bound feet began to feel its freedom. At last he became distraught, for her cries awoke other cries he still struggled to forget, and he roused the whole inn by shouting at her like a madman, 'Be quiet! I canna endure your mewling!' She froze in terror and her sobs stopped.

*

Now Peony began to share with McLennan the life of a wandering soldier.

At first her feet hurt more unbound than bound, and she couldn't walk at all. Grumbling fiercely, he had to carry her on his back, or pay another to carry her. Her feet had to be dressed and wrapped afresh each evening. The pain was so terrible that sometimes she tried to bind them again to stifle it, but her master wouldn't let her.

'They must mend,' he kept saying. And as if obeying his will, little by little, they began to. After a few months she could walk again and he bought her new shoes and some new clothes, for her old ones were threadbare and she was growing out of them.

She became a kind of mascot to the other men. They at least were not dead to pity, and they were far from their own families, so they made a pet of her; but McLennan treated her as what he felt her to be – a slave, bought and paid for.

Even before she could walk again, he put her to work. She had to rub his leather shoes with pig-grease. When his clothes got too filthy or stained with blood, she had to wash them, kneeling beside the tub. When his beard grew too long, she had to cut it with the sharp knife he called a *dhu*. If she didn't do this very carefully, he would roar at her and even try to strike her.

Usually she dodged his hand, but occasionally a blow landed. She accepted this so meekly that he felt an unaccustomed sense of shame, but he soon shook it off. She must learn to obey and do her work properly, to make up for her shortcoming.

Her main task was to brew tea for him. He liked tea in the

morning, and with his meals. She noticed he didn't enjoy his food. This was good for her, because she ate what he left. She was given no meals of her own. It didn't occur to McLennan that a body so small needed more than scraps. But the other men fed her titbits when McLennan's back was turned, so she had enough, and her feet began to uncurl and grow again. She still walked badly – her feet could never completely recover – but she could walk, and with far less pain than before.

Because she had had a hard life with nothing but bare necessities, none of this seemed very terrible to her. The worst thing – when the pain in her feet got less – was all the noise and the fighting, the blood and the raucous voices of the men, especially when they'd been drinking, all of which frightened her.

Of course she was terribly homesick for her sisters, and for the safe, simple life she'd known, but when she thought of her mother she had conflicting feelings. Her mother had been merciless about the foot-binding, telling her that she must bear the pain so that one day, when she had tiny, enchanting feet like lotus-buds, she could live the life of a rich man's wife, and help them all.

In any case, as the small army moved farther away, she

sensed that she was never going to see them again. In the nights, when she curled up in some corner on a pile of hay or even the bare ground, the tears would come. But now she didn't let her master see them.

As for Bruce McLennan, sometimes as the weeks went by he caught himself glancing at her and wondering, 'Why did I buy her?' The only answer he allowed himself was, 'At home I have servants. A laird should have someone to attend him.' He had obeyed an impulse, the random, greedy impulse that makes a man buy something just because he can.

But why this one, why not some strong, big-foot girl or young lad who would be of more practical use? Deep down he sensed a dark mystery in it. Deep down, where his feelings lay as twisted and out of shape as the girl's feet, was a connection between this little Mi-Ki and his children's voices, cut short long ago. Now, instead of his own children, he owned the child of some other man, some dead foreigner whose children had, however wretchedly, survived. McLennan owned her and he could do as he liked with her. It was a warped way of expressing what could not otherwise be expressed – the fundamental loss that can never be made up, and so must be compared to something small and contemptible, not a loss at all. The fact that she was damaged goods somehow locked into that need.

*

There was one old soldier who tried to get to know the foreign devil with the round eyes and hair the colour of fire. His name was Li-wu and he was different from the others. He was something of a philosopher, both more learned and more curious than the other men. They just saw the foreigner as a sort of tame monster, a useful fighter. Li-wu wanted to know about him. And he was drawn through pity, but later fondness, to the little girl who attended him.

So he sat near them in the evenings and tried to teach the foreigner more words so they could talk. He even taught him some writing. Bruce McLennan found this interesting because he liked to draw, and Mi-Ki writing was like drawing pictures. He thought the characters were intriguing, but faintly absurd – why so many? Why did each 'picture' stand for an object or concept? Though scarcely literate in his own language, he knew his alphabet and that seemed to him a better system. But he learned, in order to save himself from idleness and boredom.

Peony watched this from her place at her master's side. Sometimes she would copy the characters, drawing them with a pointed stick in the hard earth. When McLennan saw her doing this, he thought, 'She's not stupid,' and felt better about his bargain. At times, when Li-wu praised her gently, he felt a sort of satisfaction. 'I own her,' he thought, 'so I take some pride in her. That's all.' That made him feel at ease. It wasn't as if he took any serious interest in her. But it disturbed him when he saw that Li-wu and the child had something like a friendship. He disliked it when she would smile up at the Chi-na man, and he would talk to her seriously in their own language and pat her shoulder.

Meanwhile, Li-wu learned too, or tried to. But it was very difficult for him to understand about the things 'Ma-kri-nan' tried to describe. Watching the foreigner with his fierce, hardhearted ways, Li-wu felt uneasy. He sat with McLennan less, and McLennan noticed.

One evening, after a skirmish in which the old soldier had received a flesh wound, McLennan unexpectedly called Peony. He made her wash Li-wu's hurt, close it with thorns and wrap it in moss and bamboo leaves. The old man watched Peony's delicate hands, and thanked her for being gentle. He said to the foreigner, 'You are lucky to have this little flower.'

He shrugged. 'No luck,' he said. 'I bought her. She's mine.'

'Still you are lucky,' said the old man.

'She's just a slave,' said McLennan, frowning.

'Even slaves have spirits,' said Li-wu. 'Even slaves should be kindly used.'

McLennan stared into the older man's veiled dark eyes. He couldn't read them. Was he joking? He wanted to laugh with scorn at the notion that slaves had souls, but something stopped him. He felt uncomfortable. He was not used to feeling uncomfortable and it made him angry.

'Enough!' he barked suddenly, making Peony jump with fright. 'Be off!' He raised his hand to her and she scuttled away into the shadows of the buffalo shelter where they were.

'Your spirit is far from enlightenment,' said Li-wu quietly. And he turned away and lay down to sleep.

McLennan felt uneasy. But he put it from him. What did he care what an old Mi-Ki thought of him? He didn't belong here, he was just entertaining himself – challenging himself – among these people. He was a Scottish laird! While he lay here in this barn, a fine castle was rising on a hilltop – a castle with battlements, a moat, a drawbridge...

A castle with a dungeon.

Chapter Five

五

The private armies marched on foot. There were no horses except for the officers. There were days, sometimes weeks, with no fighting, nothing to do. The life McLennan was living seemed to get harder, and, as it became routine, to lack the excitement and satisfaction it had had at first.

He thought it a pity, perhaps, that he had opted for the life of a soldier. As an object of curiosity, he might have inveigled himself into the life of the rich here, the elegant, idle, embellished life. But then he might be shamed by these exquisite Mi-Kis with their wealth, their beautiful houses and objects, their flowered gowns and and tiny-footed women hiding behind fans and screens. Laird or no laird, gold or no gold, he was a rough man, without refinement, and he felt his appearance and manners would be out of place, as he was not out of place, ever, in his own country, where his rank would always be respected.

He was growing weary of Chi-na. As he became more used to the life, the customs and the language – and even the food, at last – he began to fear that he was losing his real self. Forgetting that he was better than these Mi-Kis. Becoming, almost, one of them. He began to think more and more about home.

It was midwinter and the countryside was bleak and cold; the nights were particularly bitter. Once something happened that disturbed McLennan very much. He woke, half-frozen, in the morning to find himself uncovered. He looked around, and saw Peony curled up under his own grimy, padded cotton quilt.

He snatched it off her, roaring, 'How dare ye, ye thieving wee nanny-goat?' She cowered, shaking her head piteously. He was about to strike her, when Li-wu intervened.

'You put it on her yourself,' he said. 'I saw you.'

McLennan was shocked to dumbness. In his sleep, had he somehow acted so contrary to himself?

'Why would I?' he muttered. 'One might as well wrap up a dog!' Li-wu just looked at him. 'I must ha' been drunk.'

'You may be a better man than you think,' said Li-wu.

McLennan set his jaw. To him, 'better' meant 'soft' and 'soft' meant 'weak'. He resolved not to drink rice-spirit or millet beer with the other men, if it made him do stupid, unwary things. He took his anger out on Peony, and Li-wu, seeing this, regretted his remarks, and refrained from saying what he was thinking – that McLennan had some feelings for the child that he refused to acknowledge.

*

Early one morning after a bloody skirmish in which he had received a wound that, while not serious, gave him nauseating pain and a sleepless night, McLennan watched dawn break in a sullen sky and knew he had had enough. He reckoned he had been away for three years. His castle must be nearly finished. It was time to go.

He looked at Peony, curled up under some straw. Should he take her? Her feet were much better now, and she served him well, but on a journey she could be a burden to him. On the other hand, who would make his tea, fetch and carry and tend his wants if he left her here? Fleetingly he thought of how she had washed and anointed and bound up his wound, only yesterday, the elfin touch of her small, gentle fingers... He shook her awake and pulled her upright.

'Pack, we're leaving,' he ordered in a terse undertone.

He pointed to his few belongings. Rubbing her eyes, she stuffed them into his bundle. He jerked his head to the doorway and walked away from the sleeping soldiers.

Peony looked back once. The old soldier, Li-wu, lay asleep. She wanted to say goodbye to him. He had been kind to her. He had taught her more than just a little reading and writing.

He had told her, 'We pass through this world many times. This hard life will pass. You will have others. In one of them perhaps you will reach Nirvana, where one is free of desires. Be righteous and patient and seek nothing for yourself. Don't hate your master, even when he ill-treats you; pity him, for he has a young soul, and if I am not mistaken, he has suffered greatly.'

Peony tried to follow this advice. It was easy not to hate McLennan, if for only one reason – he had unbound her feet. She knew that for whatever reason, he'd saved her from a life where every step would have been an agony, and where she would have been something worse than a man's servant – a man's plaything. For this she could accept her master and absorb his changing moods and even his occasional blows, which hurt her heart more than her body. For the rest, she learned to stifle fear and not to want anything too much. She tried not to think of herself at all. Now, as 'Ma-kri-nan' strode out of the camp, she followed behind, carrying his things on her back.

She couldn't know that she was leaving her homeland forever.

*

McLennan and Peony found one of the caravan routes to the west, and waited in a village for several weeks until one came by. Here the local dialect completely defeated the Scotsman and he found himself dependent on the child to communicate all his wants. She ordered his food and invariably tasted it first and even sent it back if it was too spicy or otherwise not to his taste. She arranged their lodgings and made sure that all was clean and comfortable according to what she knew, by now, he liked. Early on she had a serious quarrel with an innkeeper – the man was tightfisted with the tea leaves and served what was little more than hot water.

On this occasion McLennan stood aside and watched as the child stood toe to toe with a man twice her height and harangued him fiercely, flinging the watery brew at his feet. McLennan was astonished. She had always seemed so meek, but now he saw fire in her. In the end the man stepped aside and let Peony make the tea herself. She approached McLennan carrying it, with the light of triumph scarcely hidden in her downcast eyes. For his part he couldn't hold back a broad smile at this little thing, fighting his battles. He wanted to say something to her – he felt the need to praise her, to thank – but no. The shadow of Li-wu flitted across his mind and was banished. A slave is a slave. She had done no more than her duty.

After several weeks of shared silences which – however hard he tried – were not entirely uncompanionable, the day came when the innkeeper summoned him to the low doorway of the inn. A caravan was coming! At last! McLennan showed his teeth in excitement at the approach of the swaying camels laden with carefully packed boxes and bales of Middle Kingdom treasures, the men, foreigners like himself, trudging beside them. To these cameleer-traders he paid over some of the last of his gold coins to be allowed to join them.

At first they refused to take Peony, showing by signs that she would be a burden and would only die on the way. But McLennan negotiated, and paid more, and after much argument one of the men shrugged, laughed, lifted her up on to a camel and tied her there.

They set off. By day this man whose camel she rode made her wear a straw hat, and by night he wrapped her in sheepskin. McLennan felt irritated by these attentions, and at the same time, a strange sense of relief. But he said nothing because he didn't want Peony to die, and to treat her with such consideration would be beneath his own dignity. But sometimes at night when she crept away from the fire and curled up against the side of a recumbent camel to sleep, a vagrant sense of rightness lurked in his mind when he thought of her warm and safe and sheltered from the wind.

The Silk Road took them across deserts and through forests and over mountain passes. There were extremes of heat and cold, and food was sometimes scarce. If Peony had not been by this time sturdy and enduring, she would not have survived that journey. But after the fighting and the blood, the squalid bivouacs and the rowdy, drunken men, this was not such an ordeal for her. It was better than life with the soldiers.

After she got used to the swaying gait of the camel, and stopped being so afraid of falling off, she began to enjoy travelling. They lived mainly outside in the fresh air. There was no fighting or killing – other than game – and after some weeks of travel, the caravan moulded itself into a community of which she was a part. Every day she saw many strange things and many beautiful vistas and wild creatures. Also, there was a lot going on in her head, with so little to do but think and dream.

She remembered Li-wu saying, 'Store beauty. Furnish your memory with it. It will turn your mind into a beautiful garden that you can visit when things in the real world are hard or ugly.' A garden in her mind! Yes. She could do that.

It was strange, even to her, to find that she knew something of what a garden must be. Ever since Li-wu had mentioned the word, there had been, in her head, some shapes, shadows, like memories of a dream. She'd asked him once, 'Do gardens have...' She'd groped, trying to pin down a shadow, '...buildings in them?' And he'd replied, 'Yes.' 'And – trees?' 'Yes.' 'And bridges? Why should there be bridges?'

So he told her. A garden has four elements: water, trees, stones, and pavilions. 'What's a pavilion?' she had asked, and he'd told her that a pavilion was like a small house which was not for living in but for leisure, a place to relax, to meditate, to enjoy beauty. To listen to music. To be fulfilled.

And at once she'd remembered.

No... how could it be remembering when she had never seen a rich man's pleasure garden? Yet she knew. She knew, as surely as if she had once enjoyed the marvels of such a place: stolling, reclining, trailing her hand in a pool, listening to birdsong and sweet instruments being played, gazing about her... Her eyes, her hand, her ears, her feet (perfect feet, these, not crippled) remembered.

It was still vague and shadowy, and she hadn't thought about it very much during the time she'd been with the soldiers. But now, as, perched high on the camel's back, she crossed the wide stretches of desert, forest and mountain, she did think about it. She thought intently. She sought her garden among the shadows that mysteriously lurked at the back of her mind, or memory, or imagination... She built on the shadows. She created a magical garden out of the sights she saw in nature.

The mountain shapes became the lumps of pierced stone, which in rich men's gardens – Li-wu had explained – had been chiselled into rough, pleasing shapes, and then left in a running river for years to be worn smooth. From the trees of the forests, she picked out special ones for her garden, the small ones with twisted branches and long, dark needles and pointed cones. She shrank a lake they passed, making it into a small, placid pond, and filled it with red and white carp (oh, surely that was a memory, she saw them so clearly!) swimming lazily amid the waxy lotus flowers.

The squalid huts and tents of nomadic villages could not be recruited as pavilions, so she 'built' her own, fit to be the centrepiece of her enchanted garden. It had lacquered red pillars, beautifully carved, and fretted wooden balustrades to lean on and gaze at the beauty around her; on the pavilion walls she set scrolled hangings with paintings on them of birds, rivers, mountains and blossoms. She had music playing from musicians invisible within the pavilion. This part was easy because there were musicians of sorts among the cameleers, who played on flutes and drums and stringed boxes with bows, strange half-toned tunes that floated through the night air as she nodded half-asleep at McLennan's side after the evening meal. It was so easy to retreat to her garden then.

Evil spirits, she knew, could not move except in straight lines, so she made sure that the paths meandering through her garden were full of sinuous curves, that the bridge leading over the pond to her pavilion went zigzag.

Finally she added dragon carvings on the curved roof-corners. Her own teahouse home had had those, and of all the things she put into her magic garden, she loved the dragons best of all. Swaying on the camel's hump or huddled in her sheepskin at night, she talked in her head to her dragons. They didn't reply in words, but she could read their thoughts. These blended with the words of Li-wu, reinforcing his messages.

*

After some weeks, there was a food crisis. The nomadic tribes that normally provisioned the caravans by way of trade became scarce; in the desert they were passing through, there was a shortage of game. At night when they camped, the men held anxious conferences in their tents and around the fire. At last it was decided to take a detour to a small town across one of the passes in the mountains where, some said, food might be bartered. If this failed, they might have to turn back, or explore farther south, off the caravan route, into perilously unknown territory.

Two days' hungry journey up a steep gradient and down the other side brought them in sight of a walled desert township. Seen from above, it looked to McLennan as if it might hold four or five hundred souls. There was movement to be seen in the streets and he was hopeful; but the cameleers began shouting to each other as they came closer, and the caravan halted, still some distance above the town.

'What? What?' McLennan asked.

'See, they run about in fear! They are closing the gates! We shouldn't stay here, some evil is coming!' the cameleers were saying.

McLennan stared all around. Far away in the distance, on the plain that stretched beyond the town, he saw a sign that he understood so well that he froze at the sight of it – a dust cloud with a dark shadow running ahead of it.

'Look! It's an army riding on the town!'

There was a moment's silence as they all followed his pointing finger. Then they broke into cries and gestures of frantic alarm.

'The Mongols! The Mongols are coming! Turn the camels, run, run!'

In a frenzied scramble of movement, they tugged their beasts' heads around and began to climb back up the mountain toward the pass they had just crossed. The path was steep, and stones and shale slipped under the camels' padded feet. The men were so unmanned by fear they were not careful; many of them stumbled or slid back down the slope. Others urged and screamed at the camels, dragging on their heads; unaccustomed to hurrying, the camels hung back, uttering their strange gurgles of protest, their heads thrown up, their feet braced.

One such was the camel that carried Peony.

McLennan, himself not far from panic, glanced back – not to look for his little slave but instinctively, to see if they were being pursued – and saw the man who had charge of Peony drop the lead rope and run away up the mountain, looking so comically terrified that McLennan might have laughed at any other time.

The camel gave a last rebellious snort and then stood still in the flux of men and animals around it. Peony, gripping the wooden burden-frame, seemed paralysed, hunched over, her eyes tightly shut.

McLennan stopped.

Terrified cameleers and their stampeding animals pushed him off the rocky trail, thrusting him aside, rushing by him. He stood behind a rock and stared back, his eyes moving between Peony perched aloft and the scene far below. The invading horde had reached the gates and were swarming around the walls, surrounding the doomed town.

'Lucky for us it's the town they're after. If they knew what rich pickings there are on these beasts, they'd come after us, no doubt.' He thought of the wealth the camel carried. Yes, that was what interested him, surely – not the little frightened girl clinging there like a kitten stuck in a tree on top of the silks and the fine, well-wrapped porcelain and the boxes of tea. Of course it was to save the valuable goods that he slid and scrambled back to the abandoned camel and grabbed its rope after the rest of the caravan had gone.

When they had regrouped on the safe side of the pass, the cameleer who had abandoned Peony's mount crept back and tried to take the rope out of McLennan's big fist.

'I'll see ye roast in hell first!' shouted the Scot, threatening to knock him down. 'It's mine now, for if I hadna gone back, the beast would still be standing there, with ma wee slavie on its hump!' The man whined and pleaded and called on Allah; when that failed, he appealed to his comrades for support, but they only laughed at him. Several of the men had abandoned their camels, and there was considerable bickering, and some serious brawling, over the loads. But in the end the caravan set off again, hungrier than ever.

Fortunately, within two days they passed into a green valley to which the surrounding mountains gave rainfall, where the famine had not struck, and there the famished travellers managed to secure food supplies.

*

Now McLennan had a camel of his own and the wealth it carried. This put him in a good humour, and as usual Peony caught the overspill of his mood. He let her keep her sheepskin, and gave her adequate rations as well.

'I didna go back for *you*, mind!' he said jovially one night when she brought him his tea, brewed over the communal campfire. 'But ye brought me luck, just the same.' And he put a titbit of roast pheasant into her mouth and even patted her on the head, as one might pat a dog. If he left his hand there a moment too long, and then almost snatched it away, there was no one to take note of it.

But she had felt the warmth of his hand for once, instead of the sting of it. She went to sleep happy, and had a strange dream. She dreamed she invited her father – so long dead that she scarcely remembered him – into her garden, that they strolled there together along the patterned pebble paths with her hand in his, and that he admired her work. But when she tried to show him the dragons, pointing upward to them guarding the roof-corners, they turned their grotesque but beloved heads away. 'Please look, it's my father!' she cried out, but then, looking herself at her companion, she saw that he was bearded and huge and not her father at all. But she kept her grip on his hand just the same, as if, were she to let it go, some wild wind would sweep her away.

Chapter Six

At long last they reached the shores of the Mediterranean.

They had travelled west by the southern route. They were not in Constantinople, but in St. Jean d'Acre, in what Christians called the Holy Land – the goal of the Crusaders, who had come here in waves till late in the last century to commit hideous slaughter upon the infidel. A great castle, that these 'soldiers of Christ' had built there some two hundred years before, stood up against the sea and sky. While waiting for a ship, McLennan sold his camel, and they spent several nights in a sort of makeshift inn in the castle crypt. During the days, McLennan wandered around the narrow, malodorous lanes of the market, Peony at his heels.

There was so much to see! She was briefly tempted by the

overflowing stalls of fruit and nuts and sweetmeats – so easy for quick little hands to snatch. But Li-wu had said, 'Never take what is not yours. That which is stolen may fill the mouth with sweetness, but it burns holes in the spirit.' It never occurred to McLennan to buy her a treat, but he bought nuts and sweetmeats for himself and – a novelty which caught his eye – a folded sheet of dried rolled apricot, as big as an apron. He couldn't finish it, and it was attracting flies, so he tossed her the last strip, still marked by his teeth. The sour-sweet, 'orange' taste and the delicious chewiness made the saliva flood her mouth, but the fact that he'd given it to her, however carelessly, flooded her mind, too, and her smile broke through every time his eye fell on her. But something in that smile made him scowl and look quickly away.

*

McLennan could hardly wait for a ship for England. He put the word about, and every night would go back to the harbour beyond the great Crusader walls, and besiege the captains for news. The sight of the Crusader castle had made his own castle more vivid in his mind, made his eagerness for it sharper, and there was far to go yet! It seemed to his impatient nature, now he was on his way, that he would never get there, never see his castle or take possession of it.

Sometimes when he'd been drinking the powerful local spirit, with its strong, exotic taste of aniseed, he got drunk enough to talk to Peony as they sat on folded sacks on the stones of the crypt, with their backs to the boxes containing McLennan's appropriated goods.

'It'll be waiting – the grandest castle – not as big as this one, maybe, but big enough! Aye! Big enough!' Though she understood most of his speech now, she was not sure she followed his meaning, even when he slapped his hands on the stone walls the Crusaders had built and said, 'Castle, girl! Like this! Like this!'

'Castle like this?' she said softly.

'Aye! It's my home, ye ken! My home! My refuge! My fortress! From it I shall get my revenge at last! He shall pay, by God, I say he shall pay for what he did to me and mine!' And once, in this drunken state, he put his big head in her lap and cried. When he remembered this the next day he was so ashamed of his maudlin weakness, and her witnessing it, that he didn't speak a word to her all day. What he didn't remember was that she had stroked his greying hair and wept with him for the sorrow that had broken him, whatever it was. She knew it must be a great sorrow for him to behave as he did, showing his soft side only when he was in drink.

*

At last he found a ship, and for once didn't bargain, but paid the captain all his camel-money and gold besides, to take him and his slave-girl to England.

At first the ship sailed the smooth blue waters of the Mediterranean, and McLennan felt sure that his seasickness had been conquered. But as soon as they passed the Straits of Gibraltar and entered the Atlantic, the grey waves rose, and with them McLennan's gorge. He lay below, his stomach heaving. He groaned and cursed and lashed out at anyone who came near him, crying out for tea.

Peony set off to explore the ship. A Lascar seaman took pity on her, and smuggled her into the hold. There, crawling perilously in the torch-lit darkness over the boxes and barrels, she managed to locate McLennan's goods, which had been the last to be loaded before the ship left Acre. With the Lascar's help, she made a small hole in one of the tight-sewn sacks and extracted a small box of tea.

Next she found the galley, and with signs and smiles coaxed the ship's cook to let her make a brew. When his back was turned, she took a little honey from the ship's store. For her master, it didn't count with her as stealing.

McLennan knocked the first cup from her hand. She waited for a lull in his vomiting, then brought him another. This time he drank noisily — the vomiting had dehydrated him — let the cup roll from his hand, and slept.

She cleaned the floor, then sat at the side of his bunk and watched him. McLennan was all she had as a companion; she utterly depended on him. But she didn't imagine he depended on her. If he thought of her at all, she supposed it was as something he owned, something to serve his needs. Believing this caused her a deep, dredging sadness. But she knew sadness was bad for her spirit. She tried to push it away. She wouldn't let anger and bitterness into her heart. Instead, her small hand reached out by itself to touch the wild red beard she had so often trimmed.

More even than she needed to be cared for, she needed to care for someone. Her way of caring was to forgive Bruce McLennan all his unthinking, selfish cruelties, and remember only the good: that he took her with him when he could have abandoned her; that he rescued her when she was clinging in abject terror on the back of the camel; that he sometimes spoke a word to her that, if not kind, was at least not harsh or cold; that he had once covered her with his own quilt in the night. That in that cold stone place he called a castle, he had wept with his head in her lap. Most of all, she remembered that he had unbound her feet. These things, like the fires in the winter camps where you could warm yourself after the cold, weary days of the long march, glowed in her mind. They comforted her more than they should, for out of them and her deepest need to revere him, she made of McLennan the man he had been, once, and no longer was.

*

On shore at last in England, the Scotsman soon felt better.

He left Peony in a dreary quayside tavern while he loaded his Chi-na treasures on a hired cart and took them in to the markets of London to sell. Before he went he handed her a bale of red silk.

'Guard this,' he told her. 'Don't ye go leaving dirty fingermarks on my silk! I'm taking this back to Scotland with me to make sheets for my bed. I fancy sleeping in luxury after these years of hardship.' He grinned suddenly. There wouldn't be another laird in all Scotland who slept on silk sheets! And the colour! The brilliant red would brighten his chamber and remind him of his travels.

Peony was alone for two days. If the innkeeper's wife

hadn't taken pity on her, and brought her some bread sopped in hot milk – the dregs of what her children had had – Peony would have been very hungry as well as lonely and cold.

She had never eaten with a spoon in her life, and her eating sticks, carefully preserved throughout the long journey, couldn't pick up the soggy bread. She gave up trying, and brought the bowl to her lips. The innkeeper's wife pulled a face.

'What a little pig-dog it is, lapping its food! What foreign gutter d'you suppose the big Scots lummox found that in?' Peony couldn't understand an accent so different from the one she was used to, but she understood she was being sneered at. Hungry as she was, she laid the bowl down half-full.

When McLennan came back, he was full of vigour, and had had new clothes made. He had done well selling his goods, and his leather purse once again chinked with sovereigns. He had bought a big, strong horse, and now packed his few things, including the red silk, some Chi-na cups and several boxes of tea, into large saddlebags. He couldn't wait to get home! He hiked Peony by the arm on to his horse behind him and together they crossed the Thames on a ferry and began the last part of their long journey to Scotland.

*

As often as possible Bruce McLennan put his horse to a gallop. He didn't trouble himself about Peony who had never sat on a horse before, who had no saddle or stirrups to steady her and whose short legs were stretched across the horse's great flanks, with the lumpy saddlebags digging into her. It was worse than the camel, much worse! The camel's hump had merely swung and rocked and gyrated as it walked sedately along. The horse went like the wind in a thunder of hooves, with clods of earth and grass flying around Peony and sometimes dealing her bruising blows. She clung to her master with all her strength. She hid her face in his back and struggled with her fear.

Once it overcame her. They were riding across a desolate moor. She peeped around her master and saw a big dry-stone wall looming ahead. The horse rose up, then plunged downward. Peony was so frightened she fainted as they landed. McLennan felt her slip from the horse's back and fall to the ground.

Cursing, he pulled the horse up. He turned his head to look. He could see her lying near the wall he had jumped.

She didn't move. A pang of unlooked-for, sudden anxiety struck him, mingled with impatience. He dragged the horse's head round and rode back.

He jumped off and picked her up. She stirred in his arms, and looked up at him with those black, unreadable eyes of hers. She moved her hand as if to touch his face. He jerked his head aside before she could.

'So you're aw'richt,' he said, too loudly. 'If ye dunna like the jumps, keep those half-eyes of yours shut altogether! And hold on tight, ye wee monkey! Next time ye come off, I'll leave ye for the buzzards!'

*

They rode on, stopping at inns along the way. The food in England seemed delicious to Bruce McLennan, and he ate hugely. To Peony it was almost inedible. Despite her rough life, she was a dainty eater. She couldn't pick up these big hunks of meat with her chopsticks, and to use her hands as McLennan did was unthinkable. Other unfamiliar foods she couldn't touch. They didn't seem to her like food. Only the sweet puddings tasted good, but she got precious few of those, for McLennan still paid for nothing special for her.

But she thought of old Li-wu's words, 'Hunger doesn't

Chapter Six

matter. It's not important. The spirit needs no food.' She
survived on scraps as she had for years.

*

As they crossed the border between England and Scotland,
McLennan began to ride faster. His horse went lame, but he
drove it on till its heart failed. When it felt the whip, it bolted
forward, tried to rear up, then stumbled and fell. Its rider
flew over its head and crashed to the ground.

Peony fell with him. The searing terror as she left the
horse's back ended with a thump as she landed on top of
McLennan. She was stunned, not hurt, but McLennan was
groaning and cursing. She scrambled up, looking round first
at the horse, which lay ominously still. Next, she looked
down at McLennan, and gasped with dismay. His bare leg
below his new kilt had an angle to it that no leg should have.

Peony began to pant with fear like a frightened cat. She
stared all around. Not far away was a little stone cottage in a
dip in the moor, with smoke coming out of its chimney.
Peony didn't stop to think. She ran down the slope, falling
and rolling twice and scrambling up again, and when she
reached the low wooden door under its deep lintel, hit it
with the flat of her hand.

An old woman came. She stared in amazement at this

black-haired, slant-eyed, flat-nosed little creature, dressed in filthy rags.

'Who are ye? What d'ye want?' she croaked fearfully, half-closing the door.

'Master!' cried Peony in her high, fluting voice. 'Bad hurt! You come!'

The woman hesitated. Then she called back into the house.

'Hamish! Come quick and see this!'

Soon a young man came. He, too, stared unbelievingly at Peony. She started back up the hill, beckoning urgently. As if he couldn't help himself, he followed her.

He found the horse dead and McLennan semi-conscious from pain. Hamish lifted him with difficulty, and hung him over his shoulder. The injured leg dangled at an unnatural angle. Sick and frightened, Peony nevertheless remembered her responsibilities. With great difficulty, she untied the saddlebags from the horse and half-carried, half-dragged them after the young man, back to the cottage.

The old woman didn't want to let her in.

'Och, tak' it awaw, Hamish! 'Tis nothing human, 'tis a moor witch! 'Tis her made the horse fall, most like, and she'll bewitch us both!' she cried, hiding her crinkled face in her hands but peeping through her fingers in irresistible curiosity.

Her son brushed past her, laid McLennan on a straw-stuffed mattress and began, straining and grunting, to pull his leg straight. McLennan let out a terrible scream and a string of oaths. 'Bring warm watter and cloths and some wood for a splint,' Hamish ordered his mother.

Peony, her very skin a-creep from her master's screech of pain which she could almost feel in her own flesh, looked about her in terror. There was only one room in the cottage, with beds in box-like openings in the walls. There was a fire burning. Peony, suddenly feeling deathly cold from the long ride and from shock, edged towards it. After a scared glance over her shoulder at McLennan, now lying in a dead faint, she crouched down near the saddlebags, hugging herself, staring into the glowing heart of the flameless peat fire. It was as if, without McLennan's will, she became a figurine without life of its own.

All the time the old woman was helping her son to set the stranger's leg she watched the 'moor witch' fearfully, waiting for her to lay a spell on them. But Peony just crouched there and shivered. After a while the old woman got her courage and common sense back. When you didn't look too closely at the strange colouring and alien features, this visitation looked no worse than any half-starved child. She went to the fire and ladled something out of a pot hanging from a hook, poured it into a rough wooden bowl, and held this out to Peony at arm's length, as if to an animal that might bite.

Peony took the bowl and drank from it. It was hot mutton stew, and though it tasted very strange to her, it was good. In the bottom of the bowl were bits of vegetables and soft grains of barley. They looked quite like rice. Peony got out her chopsticks and picked the bits up delicately and ate them, leaving the meat.

'Och, Hamish, look how it eats as dainty as a fairy wi' two sticks!' cried the old woman. And she laughed, suddenly hearty and fearless. 'Just as I told ye, 'tis no witch at all, 'tis naught but a wee lassie! What were ye frichtening me for?'

*

Bruce McLennan and Peony stayed at the cottage while his leg healed. He champed and seethed with impatience. But secretly Peony was in no hurry to leave.

The old woman had taken a fancy to her.

'Poor wee'un, she's been clemmed, and not just for food,' she said shrewdly to her son. 'She's been taken frae her mither too young. She's fair starved for a bit o' love.'

The young man grunted. He was more interested in the man. He had a look about him of someone of importance. Surely there'd be a reward for helping him.

One night when his mother and the strangers were asleep, the young man got up quietly and went to investigate the man's packs, which were stacked in a corner. He opened them cautiously by the light of a candle, watching all the time the big man's sleeping shape. Inside one he found a strange object wrapped in clean linen. It must be something precious! He carefully took it out, laid it on the floor, and unrolled it a little. As the shining red stuff suddenly spilled out like blood from a wound, he snatched his hands away as if they might defile it, sat back on his heels and stared at it. It was something rare, something almost magical.

At first he was scared to touch it, but after a few moments of just looking at the way its folds caught the candlelight with subtle gleams and glints, he first stroked it very lightly and then, growing bold, lifted it on the palm of one hand and rubbed it between his blunt fingers.

It was the most beautiful cloth he had ever seen. If his mother could see it, all her superstitions would revive – she would say it was fairy-stuff, woven by the tiny fingers of the

Little People. At the same time, as a woman, however old, she would not rest until she had it for herself.

'As a man might kill for a sheet of gold,' Hamish thought, 'a woman might for this. She'd gi' her heart for it, too.' His brain, dulled by drudgery and poverty, was suddenly afire with images of taking his sweetheart this fancy bundle as a betokening gift. But how could it happen? Glancing at the stranger, whose temper he had already seen many signs of, he could see no way, and with a heavy, silent sigh, he wrapped up the silk and stowed it as it had been before.

'Aye, but I was richt,' he said. 'He's a rich man for sure. None else could afford such fine stuff.' And he crept back to bed with his mind full of hopes.

*

Peony tried not to be a trouble. She helped where she could around the cottage, and slept curled up by the fire. She tended her master, and made him his tea. He would let no one else dress his wound. The old woman's heart was touched by her devotion. She thought secretly that Peony might be the stranger's daughter by some foreign woman.

One night after their supper of rabbit stew, watching Peony washing the pots, she suddenly gave way to her motherly feelings. She scooped the child on to her lap and began to croon to her.

Peony hardly knew what was happening. When her own mother had taken her on her knee it was only to rewind the bandages on her feet, tighter than before... At first she instinctively stiffened and even struggled a little. But the old woman's body was warm and soft, her arms were tender. Peony felt as if a great need in her had been satisfied. She nestled against the old woman, and fell asleep like that. The old woman sat with her, rocking, singing softly, dreaming of her own children, when she was young.

Later she carried Peony to her own bed and they slept cosily together under some rough woollen blankets. In her sleep Peony dreamed she had reached Nirvana, the Buddhist heaven, a place of celestial comfort and peace, where there were no more needs or wants.

Chapter Seven

The delay in getting home put Bruce McLennan into a bad temper.

As soon as his leg would take any weight, he told Hamish to cut him a walking stick and began to shuffle around the room. He ordered the old woman about, and roared at her. She was not frightened of him, but she was angry. How dared he, after all they had done?

'Why d'ye let him speak to me like that!' she scolded her son. 'Why d'ye no' tell him to show some respect?'

'Be quiet, Mither. Harsh words break nae bones. I know what I'm about.'

That night when McLennan had fallen asleep, the old woman tried to talk to Peony.

'Your master is a cruel, hard man,' she said.

'Hard man,' repeated Peony sadly, nodding.

'So why d'ye stay wi' him?'

Peony couldn't answer at first. It was such a difficult question. But at last she said, 'I belong him.' Then she nodded. Yes, that explained it.

'Is he your father?'

Peony stared at her, remembering her dream. 'He buy me,' she said.

The old woman reared back her head, shocked. 'Och, that's terrible! How can a Christian buy a wee'un? I tell ye what. I'll hide ye. I can say ye've run off. Then when he goes, ye can stay here wi' us,' coaxed the old woman. 'We'll take care of ye, won't we, Hamish?'

Hamish said, 'Don't be foolish, Mither. It's my thinking he's some laird. He can help us or harm us. We must do his bidding and not anger him or steal what's his.'

The old woman hugged Peony to her side. There were tears in her eyes. But she said no more. She knew her place — her son was master.

*

McLennan watched the softness between Peony and the old woman with growing unease. It made him angry to see

Peony treated as a child of the house. He was afraid she'd want to stay with these people, that their kind treatment might make her rebellious, or at least discontented, and that thought enraged him. But there was nothing he could do without making it appear, even in his own eyes, that the child mattered to him.

One day he went outdoors for half an hour, to try how his leg would manage on rough ground. When he came back in, he noticed a strange smell. He looked around, and there were Peony's clothes, smouldering to acrid ashes on the fire, and there was Peony, shyly standing before him in a plain but neat full-length dress made of dark brown homespun wool, and a small sheepskin jerkin. McLennan got a sharp shock at the sight of her, for the clothes made her no longer look like a Mi-ki slave, but – almost like a Scottish girl. Almost like—

'What've ye done to her, woman?' he barked.

'I've dressed her in new, clean clo's, and about time, too!' the old woman retorted tartly. ''Tis time she was dressed like a proper lass.' Seeing his face darken, she began to coax him. 'Look how bonny she is, wi' her lovely black hair all smoothed and her pretty face full o' smiles!' And, indeed, McLennan saw through narrowed eyes that Peony could hardly hide her joy in wearing a new dress – a dress! She had never worn a skirt in her life, but girl-like she knew how to move in it, and she shyly picked up the fullness on each side and did a little turn to make the cloth swish.

'How d'ye expect her to do her work – or ride – got up like that?'

'I made her a skirt she can ride in. See? It's full, I didna skimp.'

'If you can sew a skirt, ye can sew trews. Make her some trews!'

The old biddy dropped her eyes and muttered, 'It's no' decent to dress her as a boy.'

'Do ye presume to teach me decency, now? Show some respect for your betters!'

The old woman faced him. 'Mr McLennan, excuse my boldness, but to my thinking, ye've been abroad for too long. Perhaps ye've forgotten how to live a civilised life. I'm not saying ye've no religion, God forbid, but it's no' right to buy and sell folk, or to treat a wee'un as if she weren't but half-human. Look at her. Only look! She's a child, sir, as it might be one of your own—'

But that was too much for McLennan. '*Be silent, woman!*' he shouted at the top of his voice, as if to blast her words away.

She shrank back, alarmed. He reached out and grabbed Peony and almost threw her against the cottage wall in his corner of the room. '*She's mine* and I'll use her as I see fit, with no interference from you or anyone, do ye understand me?'

Momentarily defeated, the old woman fled the cottage and did not return until she thought the man's temper had had time to cool. 'He's a brute and half-mad,' she thought. 'He's no' fit to have a child go near him!' More than ever she longed to rescue Peony, but how? 'I canna,' she thought hopelessly. 'I canna. God help her.'

*

There was now more tension than ever in the cottage. One day, McLennan caught Peony shyly offering the old woman some tea in one of his own cups. He rose up, and shook his stick.

'You dare to steal my tea!' he roared. 'You touch a drop and I'll knock your thieving grey head off your shoulders!'

This was past bearing! 'Keep your brown watter!' she cried, and emptied the cup on the earth floor. She would rather have thrown it in his face. ''Tis no drink for a Christian! If ma Hamish heard your abuse, he might do some knocking himsel'!'

McLennan, taken aback at her sudden fierceness, backed off, grumbling. But that night the old woman saw him strike

Peony across the face and threaten her with worse if she showed any more signs of 'forgetting her place'. She saw then that her growing fondness must be curbed, for the child's sake.

*

Hamish was away on a mission for McLennan – to buy him a horse. After a week, he came back. He had been to considerable trouble and expense. He was more sure than ever that his visitor was important, and he was anxious to please him. But he was apprehensive as he rode home, leading the new horse over the moor. The only horse he'd been able to find for him was old and sway-backed.

McLennan hurried out of the cottage when he heard the horses coming. He took one look, and flew into a rage.

'Are ye trying to insult me? Do ye expect me to ride to my castle on an old nag like this? Do ye no' ken who I am?'

'I do not,' said Hamish. 'Who are ye?'

'I am Bruce McLennan, Laird of Kinbracken! If ye dunna give me the respect that's due to me, I will make ye pay for it, never fear, when I come to my ain place!'

Hamish would have liked to throw him out of his house. But he thought of the red silk, and instead he said, 'I'm sorry, sir. I didna know. And I'm sorry the horse isna to your liking.

He was the best I could find. And,' he added, 'as for paying, I paid for him masel'. Will you kindly pay me back?' And he named a sum of money.

McLennan was so angry he lashed out at the young man with the stick. But this unbalanced him. He fell over on the floor and lay there cursing loudly.

The other three looked down at him. It was Peony who went to his side. He used her to lever himself up from the floor, clutching her so tightly she was bruised. She helped him to the bed and he lay down on it, calling for whiskey. The young man, sullen and uncertain, gave him some from his precious store, while his mother scowled furiously. Later that night, when his mother had gone to bed, the young man crept over to McLennan.

'If the horse isna good enough for ye, ye could buy mine. No' for money. I thought——'

'Well? What did that giant brain of yours *think*?' sneered his guest.

'If it happened ye had... anything valuable about ye... from abroad, maybe, y'know, something of the worth of a good horse, which he is, we could maybe——'

'Go on,' said McLennan very quietly. It was a dangerous quiet, but Hamish didn't know that.

'Strike a bargain.'

There was a long silence and Hamish felt sweat break out on his upper lip.

'Ye've been in my pack, ye sneaky young whelp,' said McLennan in the same controlled undertone that betokened fury held in check. 'If ye've so much as laid one of your mucky peasant's fingers on ma silk, I'll thrash ye to within an inch of your worthless life!' His voice rose abruptly to a bellow.

Hamish would not give way. He knew McLennan was no match for him. 'I did look, I own it, but I never besmirched it! My offer holds. Gi' me the see-ulk as ye call it and take ma good horse and let's part friends.'

McLennan put a rein on his temper. This sheep-herder was not worth it. Give him his silk? Have *him* sleep in silken sheets? The idea made him laugh aloud. 'Keep your nag,' was all he said. And rolled over and went to sleep.

*

A few days later, McLennan decided his leg was better. He ordered Peony to pack his belongings and load the old horse, and made Hamish help him on to its back.

Peony was lifted on behind him. She didn't look back at the old woman, who was standing in the low doorway. She didn't want to see her crying. Peony tried never to cry herself, but now the tears pushed at her throat and her eyes stung with the need to shed them.

Hamish, feeling angry and cheated, stood in front of the horse and held the bridle, as if he would stop McLennan from leaving.

'Have ye naught to say to me?' he muttered.

'Aye, I have,' replied McLennan loudly. 'And it's this! Let go the beast's head or I'll beat ye to the ground!' He raised his whip.

Hamish looked into his red, angry face and saw that he meant what he said. He shrank back. McLennan brought out a single sovereign and flung it on the turf at Hamish's feet. 'Stoop for it!' he said contemptuously. The whip came down on the horse's rump. It jumped sideways. Peony clung on, all her fear coming back to her.

She buried her face against her master's plaid. She never even waved back to the old woman; she dared not release her grip. The horse galloped clumsily away. Bruce McLennan shouted at it, and belaboured it. He cursed Hamish as he rode, for not buying him a better horse.

Behind them in the cottage doorway, the old woman wept and railed at her son. 'Did ye see how scared she was?

Puir mite, puir lass! I would ha' cared for her, I would ha' loved her like ma ain! Och, Hamish, your greed closed up your pity so ye wouldna let me keep the lassie, and now here y'are, left with naught at the end but a sliver o' metal and his insults to chew on. It serves ye right! I'm sore afeared the brute'll be the death of her, puir wee thing!'

*

After only two hours' journey, the wild rider began to see landmarks that he knew. His excitement grew almost unbearable. He was nearly home! An hour more and he would see if the chest of the King's gold he had given to Master Douglas had been well spent.

He lashed the horse without pity. He never gave a conscious thought to Peony. But he knew she was still there, behind him. He could feel her warm against his back, her arms tightly around him. She was clinging like a monkey, as he'd ordered. This felt right to him.

At last the sweating horse came on to a hill. Bruce McLennan drew rein. He stood there with his brand-new plaid blowing back, and caught his breath.

He could see it! There it was! Across the valley on the next crag, his castle — *his castle* — stood up against the sunset. It was just as he'd imagined! A great black shape, with towers and battlements, and below it, a large cluster of thatched houses, enclosed by a palisade, where none had been before. All due to him, there was a giant landmark, and a living settlement full of people who owed him absolute loyalty. That castle would stand forever, a monument to his power and wealth. A sight to fill an enemy or a stranger with fear, with awe, with envy. No one would dare to come against him now!

'My castle!' he breathed. 'Now I'm a true laird and none can say otherwise!'

Peony opened her eyes and peeped around his body. She saw the black shape on the opposite hill. It looked like a monstrous toad, squatting there, a toad with four horns. To him it was a dream made real. To her it was a nightmare place. It filled her with a sudden, quailing sense of foreboding.

Bruce McLennan gave a sudden loud laugh of triumph, and struck the horse. It went down the hill fast, blowing and kicking up clods, its big front hooves sliding as it tried to control its descent. Once on the flat, it crossed the valley at a gallop. He rode through the new village thunderously, bringing the people to their doors. He could hear them calling to each other, 'The Master! The Master's back!' He knew that on the battlements of his castle, the watch would see him coming.

Chapter Seven

He slowed to a trot along the dirt track between timber-framed houses, shops, orchards and little plots that had not been there when he left, filling up with pride. People were running to line the way, the men touching their foreheads, the women curtseying to him, the children wide-eyed. He passed finally his own old house, now the village hall. Next to it, a little church had been erected with a steeple and a bell. He thought of the devout days of his childhood and for a moment regretted that there would be no fine, high-ceilinged chapel with stained-glass windows to give his castle dignity and call God to his side. But for what? He refused to house or praise a God who, in his hour of greatest need, had abandoned him.

He reached the moat. The drawbridge at the end of the high ramp was being hurriedly lowered with a loud rattle of chains. He could imagine the scurrying and scampering, as of so many disturbed mice, inside the castle as dozens of stewards and maids, menservants and grooms, guards and cooks roused themselves to prepare for his homecoming.

As his horse's hooves stamped up the ramp and clattered hollowly across the drawbridge, the great portcullis on the other side of the moat was raised. Yes! Yes! It was all exactly as he had planned!

the Dungeon

As they passed along the narrow passage between the U-shaped gatehouse towers, Peony gazed up at the shadowy timbered roof. She told herself not to be afraid. It was only like going into another life, just as Li-wu had said.

Chapter Eight

Bruce McLennan rode his horse into the inner ward.

The castle was all around it. Its stone walls rose up blackly. The four towers stood against the darkening sky.

When he looked about him, he felt as near to happiness as he was capable of. Everything was the way he had wanted it. It looked just like the plan he had scratched on the slates for the master builder, three – or was it nearer four? – years ago.

There would be time to explore, to examine the many rooms, the great dining hall, the kitchens, the stables, the storerooms, the round tower rooms, one of which would be his bedchamber and one of which should have been the chapel... But there was something he had to see first. The vital thing. He dismounted, unfastening the girl's grip as if undoing a belt, and kicked his good leg over the pommel of the saddle, sliding face-out to the ground. His injured leg gave him a mighty pang, but he righted himself and handed the reins to his chief groom, a man who had crossed from youth to early middle age since he had left.

'Robert McGregor? Is it you under that grey thatch?'

The man knuckled his forehead. 'Aye m'laird. Welcome home.'

'I must inspect my dungeon!' McLennan muttered. Then he limped away.

Rob was holding the horse's reins and staring, not after his master, but at Peony. She was so tired that when she was left unsupported on the horse's back, she began to slip off. Rob was so astonished at the sight of her that he only just managed to reach out and break her fall. But he didn't like touching her. He led the blowing horse away, leaving the child on the cobbles.

Inside the stable, he prepared to hand the reins to a boy who was waiting there. He'd been peeping out over the half-door, open-mouthed, watching everything – the legendary laird, the great lathered horse, but most of all, the little lass who had ridden pillion and now lay on the stones of the courtyard like a dead thing.

Chapter Eight

'Aw'richt, Finlay,' said Rob the groom good-naturedly. 'I can see ye're dying to have a look at her. I'll rub him down for ye. But dunna be long. Take a pail, and if ye see the Master coming, draw some watter for the horse and get yersel' back in here, quick.'

Fin needed no second telling. He grabbed a pail and rushed out of the stable. He stood over Peony, looking down at her. She didn't move. He stirred her gently with his foot. She jerked, and sat up a little. Her hair stuck out around her face, stiff with dust; her eyes were almost sealed up from exhaustion and the salt from wind-summoned tears. Fin burst out laughing – he thought her the funniest thing he had ever seen in his life. He bent and peered into her face.

'Can ye see me out of those wee eyes?' he asked her.

She stared at him. He pushed her again with his boot.

'Can ye no' talk?' he asked.

She nodded.

'Say something then. Tell me your name, if ye've got one.'

'*Wo shi mudan*,' she said, as she said it so often in her head. She had no notion of what her name might be in English.

The boy said, 'Och, I canna catch that! I'll call ye Wee Eyes. Get up, lass!' He pulled her up by the hand. 'D'ye understand me?' She nodded. 'Are ye hungry?' She nodded again. 'Come on, then.'

He first drew water for the horse, then led Peony to his corner of the stable, where he slept. He dug in the straw and took out some bread and a piece of cheese kept shut in a box against the mice. She looked at them askance. Scottish food still didn't look like food to her, and besides, the box was grubby and the cheese reeked.

But Fin chose to ignore her pursed lips. He sat her down in the straw and fed her, breaking off bits of bread and cheese and pushing them into her mouth. For the first time she let herself taste a cheese that was not bland, like the yak's milk kind, but strong. It smelt so bad she could hardly swallow the first pieces, but mixed in her mouth with the bread (and her hunger) it became tolerable, then tasty.

Next, he put some into her hand, opened his mouth wide, and pointed a grimy finger into it. He wanted her to feed him, like a mother bird! What did it mean? But some dimly remembered instinct for fun awoke in her. She who had not played a game for years, recognised that he wanted to play with her. She smiled, suddenly and widely, and pushed the first bit halfway down his throat, nearly choking him.

He almost bit her fingers off. She snatched them out, and they both burst out laughing.

'There's chewing to do first, ye ken!' he said, pretending to be stern. But she knew he was not really angry. They played the game, turn and turn about, till the food was all gone and Rob the groom was in the doorway calling Fin to his duty.

'Gi' me a few more minutes!' he begged. 'I mun get her cleaned up!'

He touched Peony's golden skin, her black hair, both encrusted with the dirt of travel.

'Ye need a wash!' he grinned. 'Ye're a dirty Wee Eyes!' He pretended to scold her, the way his mother scolded him.

He took her to the well in the courtyard, and pumped some cold water into the wooden pail. Then he stood by while she washed herself. She hated to be dirty, and was grateful to him for understanding her need. She put her face down into the pail, catching a glimpse of herself as she did so. She quickly dipped her face, not letting herself examine her image for more than a second, because it frightened her. She had hardly ever seen herself and the few glimpses she got contradicted her notion of herself as a being that matched her magic garden, beautiful and radiant like the flower she was named for.

Fin watched her approvingly as she rubbed her hands over her face and neck, and rinsed the dirt away again and again till her golden skin shone. He drew more water for her to dip her hair.

When she stood before him, dripping and shining, he said, 'Have ye no clothes but these?' She shook her head solemnly. The clean new clothes the old woman at the croft had given her weren't so clean any more. But they were all she had. Then he said, 'Why dunna ye walk right?' He had noticed her strange hobbling gait. 'Are ye stiff from the ride?'

Bewildered, she tried both to nod and shake her head at once.

He passed over this. 'How did the Master find ye?'

'He buy me,' whispered Peony.

'So ye're worse off than me,' said Fin. 'I'm a tenant and a groom's boy. Ye're a true slave, bought and paid for.' He stared at her in awe. He didn't feel like laughing any more.

*

Peony's life in the castle began.

Bruce McLennan had other servants now. Peony didn't have to work hard, as she had before. But he liked to know where she was – if he had not seen her for a day, he would make some excuse to summon her and give her some task to do for him. She made his tea, and served it in the small porcelain cups, without handles, that they had brought from Chi-na. Sometimes she had to polish his boots, or mend his clothes, jobs she was used to. He never spoke kindly to her, and of course never thanked her, but he didn't shout at her or try to hit her, either. He had no reason to.

He had come home and he was satisfied, for the moment. His castle put him in a good humour. Master Douglas had lived up to his reputation. Every part of the building was exactly as McLennan had planned it. And now – also according to plan – he had a much larger tenantry. Most of the men who had been recruited from other places to build the castle had chosen to stay and settle within it or near it; not only was the village growing, the surrounding countryside was now dotted with hamlets and farms. McLennan was now laird over perhaps a thousand people. For one who had started life as a poor lad in a highland fishing village, he had reason to be proud.

'I know they whispered that I was as lowborn as themselves,' he thought. 'Let them raise themselves as I have!

Let them build themselves a castle before they whisper that I'm no' a true laird!' But these thoughts about status avoided the darker motives he had had for building a fortress, for gathering able-bodied men.

*

The castle that seemed to its master the fulfilment of a dream was in Peony's eyes grim, damp and darkly cold, but it breathed a kind of safety. Sometimes as summer came, and the unambitious northern sun at last climbed overhead and shone into the courtyard, the members of McLennan's large household grew more cheerful, and, though at first suspicious of her because of her foreignness, some learned to be kind to her. It was a new life indeed, and she often thought of Li-wu. She knew that the kind of 'new life' he had told her about involved passing through the gates of death and being reborn into another body, but this sort was good enough for the moment. Living in the castle, with no war or hard riding and her master in a good temper, was better than anything she'd known since she left her family. The memories of past hardships faded.

So did the magic garden in her head. She hardly ever visited it nowadays, because she hardly needed to.

And the best of all was Fin.

Chapter Eight

She had never really had a friend. She didn't know the word. But Fin taught it to her.

'We're friends, ye ken,' he'd say. 'I'm your friend, and you're my friend. Say it.'

'Friend,' she repeated. It seemed a serious matter to her. Fin was always grinning but she was solemn and didn't always smile back. One day he put his fingers to the corners of her mouth and pulled them up.

'That's a smile,' he said. 'Ye're no' used to it. But ye'll learn. Go on. Try it. Like this, see?'

And he was so kind and funny that she began to smile more and more.

When Fin got leave, he would visit his parents' home in the countryside near the castle. He told her about it.

'It's a bonny wee hoos. Mother keeps it warm and bright and clean – ye'd like that, Wee Eyes, wouldn't ye? And she's a gie good cook! I'd make her cut things up small, so ye could eat wi' your wee sticks. She'd help to fatten ye up. Ye'd be right bonny if ye had more flesh on ye, och aye!, and if we could make your eyes round! Then I could call ye Round Eyes!'

Peony didn't understand all his talk. But she liked to listen. She learned new words. She understood her nickname and sometimes she tried to open her eyes wide. 'Round eyes!' she said.

'Aye! Ye're doing your best! But I doubt ye can ever make them come right,' he teased her. Secretly he thought her eyes beautiful and mysterious with their smooth, straight-edged lids. He would sometimes bend and try to peer into them, as if to discover what she was thinking, but she would cover them and run away.

Fin asked Peony time after time to come with him to visit his parents. But she just shook her head.

'Master not let,' she said.

'He wulna mind! He wulna know.'

Rob, Fin's boss, heard him.

'Let the lassie be, Fin, dunna tempt her. The master might kill her if she took leave.'

Fin stared at him incredulously. 'Kill her? Why would he?'

'Ye dunna ken his temper.'

'He seems quiet enough to me.'

'Aye,' said Rob soberly. 'He was quiet once, calm and good-natured – another man altogether.'

'That would be – before McInnes—'

'Hold your whisht! One day if you're unlucky, ye'll see the worst of what he's become.'

'What's the worst he could do to me?'

The groom looked at him without speaking for a while. Then he said, 'Have ye no' seen the dungeon?'

'Not — not since it was finished.'

'Well, I have. It's a terrible, terrible place. And if I'm no' mistaken, the Master would like nothing better than a prisoner or two down there. That's what he had it made for. I'd not like to see you chained up in the dark wi' the rats, wi'out even a bit o' straw to lay your silly young head on.'

*

The groom had good sense.

Bruce McLennan could not enjoy his castle without being constantly reminded of what lay under it. He didn't like the dungeon being empty. It needed its destined prisoner. Or else for what was all that digging and carrying away the spoil, and lining with stones? For what were the iron rings in the wall and the chains? What use was the big iron-clad door with the brass key? The key now hung on a nail in his bedchamber, and was the first thing he saw each morning when he woke under his red silk sheets, lit up like a reminder by the sun striking in a shaft through the narrow window. There was a connection here with his conscience and his manhood.

The years abroad had gone some way to making him, not forget what had happened, but to distance him from it to some extent. Time and new things, the fighting and the journeys – and something else that he would never have acknowledged – had softened the cutting edges of his hideous memories and his thirst for revenge.

But now the satisfaction and relief of getting home and settling into his castle, that had gone into his system like meat, was digested and absorbed, and soon he was hungry again – restless and unrelieved. The air of the Scottish moors brought scents of heather and broom and bog and the tang of sheep; the changing light brought sights that set the past before him again: the days when he and his bride climbed the crags and lay together in the hollows and embraced, and later played with their young ones and planned the future they would have together. That future that they'd planned had no castle in it, no dungeon. It was a thing of peace and prosperity for them and their children, a future destined to be broken into, despoiled and destroyed.

He spent much time up on the battlements, looking out over the countryside, a view much altered by his own endeavours. His will had brought about the village that now lay at the foot of the crag. He often stood staring down at it, watching the people who lived there. He especially liked the midweek market day, when the wagons, carts, or laden beasts from outlying farms would trundle in through the gates in the palisade, along the dirt tracks to the marketplace in the middle of the village. People would come out of their houses and flock to buy, and then would hurry back to open up their shops. On a shutter, lowered to make a counter, they would set out their goods — home-baked bread and cakes, eggs and chickens and cuts of meat, fresh-caught pike and eels from the river, vegetables, fruits, jars of honey, stone bottles of beer and wine, household wares and tools, balls of wool and homespun cloth...

His own servants would leave the castle and cross the moat into the village to mingle with the villagers, to buy supplies for his large household and no doubt to exchange news and gossip. He could hear the sounds — drifts of distant laughter and shouts, children's cries as they played, dogs barking, occasional singing or playing of instruments... On Sundays he watched the people, in their best clothes, streaming to the church. His own people, too, who had no place of worship inside the castle walls... When the wind blew in his face, he could faintly hear the hymns.

This was his village and these were his people. How easily

satisfied they were! How simple their lives! They worked hard, but they were rewarded for it. He remembered the strange sights and customs, the elegance and superiority he had glimpsed on his travels, the evil vices and filth and stench of the streets and quays of London... Here was better than either. Here, there was fresh air, fields, flocks, game, fish, crops, orchards. Self-respecting, decent folk, upheld by their simple faith... What more was needed for happiness and well-being?

And he thought, 'If I do nothing!' That was all that was needed for this to continue. These people lived in peace and sufficiency. He needed only to rule them benignly from his castle and *do nothing, change nothing, initiate nothing* and they could go on as they were, and they would tip their hats to him and teach their children to respect him, and bless him in their prayers. 'They trust me to take care of them,' he thought. 'Their lives are in my hands.'

But then a griping pain began to gnaw his vitals. He could feel it, like a rat inside him. 'If I had been left but one,' he thought. 'Only one of my dear ones to love and be loved by, then I could perhaps forgive. Then maybe I could give up my revenge and live, and let live, in peace! But he left me not one, nor hen nor chicks, not one!' And his fury would return. He would grind his teeth in his bitter aloneness, and turn his face away from those below who rejoiced in living for their families. He would climb slowly down the stone steps inside the great curtain-wall, and go to his room, and send for 'the girl' to bring him his tea. His eyes, blankly staring as his mind turned inward and backward to the beautiful, then terrible, and all unchangeable past, would not even follow her quiet passage between the door and the table at his side where she carefully laid the fragrant cup.

He would not even notice her.

*

One morning he rose from his bed with a violent jolt. He had been dreaming of those he had lost. He saw them from the battlements, coming through the village, and when they drew close his heart leapt with happiness and he shouted and called to them till his throat was sore. But they stood off from the castle, and though he ordered the drawbridge lowered to let them in, the gaping moat-ditch lay unbridged between them. They didn't look at him but stared at the gate as if waiting for him to come through it...

Later that same day, glancing from the window that overlooked the courtyard, he caught sight of Peony running across the open ward near the well, being chased by Fin.

They were there and gone in a flash. But that glimpse of her with her flying dark hair and upturned face – that free motion of happy childhood – broke his dream of the night before, and awoke such memories that he was struck almost senseless and staggered backward, stunned. When he came to himself he was standing in the middle of his chamber with his sword gripped in both hands, breathing in great gasps.

His enemy lived. Within reach of McLennan's vengeance, the villain lived out his life in peace. It must not be.

From that moment, the die was cast.

McLennan sent out spies. He instructed them not to approach the enemy's stronghold – some forty miles distant – directly. Instead they rode through several villages belonging to McInnes, where any traveller might stop to buy a tankard of ale at the tavern. They lingered there to listen to local talk. They returned to report that the neighbouring laird was not the man he had been ten years ago. He had taken to drinking too much whiskey, being often drunk from midday. Though this man, too, had a castle of sorts with strong walls, his defeat and capture should be easy.

*

Despite Rob's warnings, Peony did leave the castle to go home with Fin.

It happened when, unusually, the Master had gone away for a few days. It was rumoured he was visiting his more far-flung tenants to do a sort of census — to count how many able-bodied men he could call on to fight for him. Most lairds did this from time to time, or rather, ordered it to be done. Perhaps, Rob hinted, he wanted to make himself known to the newcomers, to assure himself of their loyalty.

'There's fighting in prospect. I'd lay a sovereign on it,' Rob said sagely.

Fin seized his moment.

'So now could I take the lassie to visit Mother?' he asked eagerly.

Rob thought about it. The girl had never set foot outside the castle walls since she arrived. She was mewed up like a prisoner. It would do her good.

'Och, go on then. But don't take risks with her. She's the Master's favourite.'

'Why d'ye say that? He hardly notices her.'

'That's all you know. If she's no' by when he wants to see her, have ye no' heard him bellow like a gored bull? She's his wee pet, if he knows it or not. He'd be lost without her.'

'He's a funny way of showing it.'

'Listen, ma lad. Let me tell ye something. When a man

has lost his wee'uns he's lost his sun and his moon. Then he needs every candle he can find to light up his dark.'

'Ye mean, Wee Eyes is his candle?'

'Aye. Without her he'd be more blundering and blind than he is, and so much the worse for us all.'

Fin was too excited at the prospect of taking Peony home to pay much attention. As if he'd take chances with her safety, anyway! He was far too fond of her, and at nearly fourteen he was already man enough to feel protective. He made her put on her new dress (made for her by one of the castle sewing-women in her spare time), wrapped her shoulders in a little shawl he'd brought for her from home as a gift, and together they walked boldly out through the castle gate and across the drawbridge, still lowered after the Master's departure.

First they walked through the village. It was a beautiful spring day. The townsfolk had opened their shops. Fin spared a few coins from the wages he was taking to his family, and bought Peony a honey cake. The people had heard about the little girl from afar (there were dark, superstitious tales about her, as well as kinder ones) and tried not to stare at her too openly. If Fin caught them glancing or whispering, he would scowl until they remembered their manners.

Chapter Eight

Soon they reached the edge of the village and went through the gate between the high earth ramparts, and into the countryside. All nature seemed to open up before the two children so long shut into the dark castle walls. As they ran up and down the hills, the tussocks of rough grass and the little ling bushes seemed to bounce back under their feet, propelling them forward like springs.

'The way it looks when the sun shines on it, and the heather all in bloom, ye'd never think how glum it seems in winter!' exulted Fin. 'Dunna ye think so? Is the land ye come from half as bonny as Scotland when it's like this?'

Peony didn't agree or disagree. She just smiled happily. Her hand was fast in his. Her free hand held up her dress so she could run better. Her feet felt almost normal now; she could forget, for long stretches, that they didn't look right. So when, after running and walking for two or three miles they came to a little stream and Fin suggested they take their shoes off and paddle, she plumped herself down on the grass and pulled off her shoes without a thought.

When Fin saw her bare feet he stopped in mid-chatter and gaped at them, open-mouthed. 'Och, lass! What happened to your toes?'

Swiftly she pulled them up under the hem of her dress.

Her face whitened and she sucked her lips into her mouth, looking at him in a scared way as if expecting him to turn from her in disgust.

'Naw, naw, don't hide them! Show me them. Come on, it's aw'richt, show me.'

Slowly, slowly, she poked the tip of one foot out. The toe-knuckles appeared first, because the ends of the toes were still turned somewhat under the foot. They would never recover from the damage done to her for the sake of men's perverse desires and the fashion of the rich and idle in her country.

Fin stared at them for a long time, then reached out both hands and took the little foot between them, stroking it softly. 'Och, puir wee foot! Puir wee foot!' he murmured. And suddenly he knelt up on the edge of the stream, bent his head down and kissed first one, and then, fishing it out of its hiding-place, the other. Peony watched him open-mouthed. His tenderness was like a forgiveness for her broken feet. It made them seem right again.

'Let's sit wi' our feet in the stream,' said Fin.

So they did. The clear, cold water chuckled past their calves and Fin said, 'If it was magic watter, it would heal you. Were ye born wi' them like that?'

'No,' Peony answered. 'Mother do, so that I am beautiful.'

Fin was bewildered. Her *mother* had done this?

'I dunna understand,' he said.

Peony frowned. It was all a long time ago. 'Mother tie my feet,' she explained. 'Tie tight to make them small-small like—' She cupped her hands together to make the shape of a lotus-bud. 'Like rich woman foot, so one day I will be rich woman.'

'How would having wee feet make ye rich?'

'Rich man marry me, give me many thing, I give many fine thing to Mother and sisters,' she answered seriously.

Fin sat in benumbed silence. Her feet had been deformed on purpose, for gain. He couldn't believe it, but he'd held the evidence in his hands. A sudden flash of insight came, into what she must have suffered. This brought another flash, of absolute fury. He put his arm around her suddenly.

'Then ye have no mother. My mother will be your mother,' he said between clenched teeth. 'We'll be brother and sister.'

'Och, ayiii!' cried Peony in her funny mix of accents, gazing at him with shining eyes as the water united their feet in its clean embrace.

They reached Fin's house by lunchtime.

He hadn't, of course, been able to warn his mother he was bringing a visitor, but she was expecting him – he came home on the same day every month, the day of the full moon, so that he could find his way back easily if the visit stretched, as it tended to, especially in winter, beyond sunset.

She was waiting for him with his favourite meal of haggis with bashed neaps, and apple pudding. The whole cottage was full of good smells, not least fresh bannock which his mother was just pulling out of the brick oven beside the woodstove.

When she turned and saw the two figures in the doorway, she almost dropped the round, flat loaf. 'Fin! Ye brought her!'

'Aye, Mother,' said Fin proudly. 'Here she is. Meet Wee Eyes.'

Fin's mother, Janet, had been married at fourteen and was still only thirty-six. She had six sons of whom Fin was next to the youngest, and no daughters. Now she looked at the child standing next to Fin ('A wee girl at last! Who'd have thought it would be my Fin would bring her!' – for Donald, her oldest boy, had not yet brought home a sweetheart) and thought she would like to run to her and give her a hug. But there was something in the tense little figure, poised like a wild creature uncertain if it was going to be welcomed or chased away, that told her she shouldn't make any sudden moves, even motherly ones.

'Did ye have a fine walk, children? Ye'll be ready for your dinner. Wash your hands, then, and come to table.'

Peony followed Fin to the water trough out at the back and Fin pumped water for her and they washed. He was grinning like a zany. She could feel his happiness. But she was not easy. What if her master should find out? What if he should come riding over the moor and clatter into this yard?

Back indoors, Fin introduced her to his brothers, the eldest first.

'This is Donald. This is Malcolm. This is Rab. This is Angus. And this wee scallywag is my young brother Jamie.'

Jamie, aged nine, was staring at her without shame.

'Why does she look so gie queer?'

'*Jamie, mind your manners!*' hissed his mother, muffling his mouth with her apron. 'I'm sorry,' she said to Peony, as the little boy struggled free. 'We don't see many visitors, but he knows better than to make personal remarks, all the same!'

Just then the father of the family entered. He was a stocky, ruddy-faced farmer with bristly grizzled hair. He'd clearly changed from his working clothes when he heard that a guest had come, and when he saw Peony he greeted her courteously, offering her the seat of honour at his right hand at the long, scrubbed table.

Peony was quite used to Scottish food by now, and this food was good. It was little tight-filled bags of some peppery meat-mixture, which, when broken open, could easily be eaten with chopsticks, and some mashed root vegetable the colour of apricots, puddled with butter. This was devoured to the accompaniment of loud masculine conversation from all sides, and when it was cleared away, Janet brought to the table a great pudding as big as an upturned wash-bowl, redolent of apple and honey but with a contradictory whiff of meat too, from the rich lambs'-kidney suet that had gone into its thick pastry crust. When it was cut into with a big knife, the cloud of fragrant steam that rose out of it drew roars of appreciation from around the table. 'Mother's best pudding, special for Fin!' said Father.

They all covertly watched Peony's way with the 'wee sticks'. There was some smirking and nudging, but a look from their father scotched it. He leant to Peony.

'Where d'ye come from, lassie?'

'Chi-na,' she said with a trace of pride. From McLennan she had learned to call her homeland by its English name.

'Where might that be?'

Chapter Eight

'Long way. *Long* way.' They all waited, eight of them round the table, staring at her expectantly. She mustered her words. 'Place where all people has hair like me. Eyes like me, too. I not just one, there. Every people has wee eyes there. There in Chi-na,' she went on seriously, as they all continued to gaze at her, 'you, all you, are "Big Eyes".' She made two circles with her fingers and thumbs.

This was the longest speech she had ever made and she was justly proud of it. So it put her out when twenty-one-year-old Donald, the eldest, threw his head back and laughed.

'What's so funny?' asked Fin, bristling.

'Och, no disrespect! She's richt!' Donald boomed. 'In her country, wherever it is, *we'd* be the ones wi' the different eyes! Ye shouldna call her Wee Eyes, Fin. That's what she's trying t'tell ye. It's rude. It's a *personal remark*. Isn't that richt, Mother?'

'Aye,' said Janet. 'Come to think of it, that's just what it is! Good for you, Donald!'

'But she dunna mind it!' said Fin, flushing bright red. Could he have been hurting her feelings all this time?

'How do ye know?' said Malcolm. 'I'd mind it, for certain, if someone called me a name that made fun of ma looks!'

'I wasna making fun!' exclaimed Fin, shocked.

'She mun have a name of her ain,' piped up Jamie.

Fin's father leant forward again and put his face close to Peony's.

'What's your name, lassie? The one ye was born to.'

'*Wo shi mudan,*' she said softly.

'That's what she always says,' said Fin.

'Washee Moodee,' said Jamie cheekily, and was hushed by his mother.

'What does it mean?' asked Donald.

'What does it mean, what does it mean!' mimicked Fin. 'What does "Donald" mean? It's just a name in her own language!'

A lively argument was about to break out. But then they saw that their little guest was doing something. She'd dipped her finger into a tankard of ale and proceeded to draw with it on the scrubbed-white wooden tabletop. The boys, who were seated far down the table, got up and crowded round to look.

'Will ye look at that! It's a flower!'

'Aye, but what kind?'

'It's like the pompom on top of a tam-o'-shanter.'

'I've never seen a flower the like o' that.'

'It must be a kind they only have in her country.'

'You should think of a pretty name for her, Fin. A flower name,' said Janet.

'Dandelion!' joked Jamie, and was hushed again by his mother.

But none of the flowers they could think of was like the flower Peony had drawn with the ale.

'You should call her "Little Flower",' said Janet.

Fin and Peony stared at her. It was a beautiful name. Fin felt ashamed he hadn't thought of it. But when he looked at Peony, he still thought 'But she'll aye be Wee Eyes to me.'

The matter of names was dropped, and after dinner the men prepared to go back to their work about the farm. It was then Fin remembered to tell them that the Master was visiting some of his tenants.

'We must have the place looking its best,' said his father. Every tenant of the estate was aware that the laird owned it and let them live on the land and farm it only so long as they wrung the last ounce of produce from it and paid their tithes.

'Rob says he's maybe doing a head count because there's fighting coming,' said Fin importantly.

The men and boys, already trooping out, stopped, and glanced apprehensively at each other. Janet stiffened and went pale.

'Well,' said her husband slowly, rubbing his chin, 'I always said, after what happened, it was bound to come. Bound to come. We're lucky to have had so many peaceful years.'

*

After a happy day playing games and doing a few chores, Fin and Peony left before the sun went down, chivvied by Janet who was worried about them getting back.

As they were leaving, Fin clutching a packet of goodies, Janet managed the hug she had been hungering to give Peony. She crouched before her with her warm arms around her and said, 'Ye're welcome to visit us every month, Little Flower. Please come again soon!'

After the children had walked some way, Peony broke the silence.

'Your mother is good woman,' she said.

'Aye, she's all of that,' said Fin warmly.

'She be my mother now truly?'

'Ye can borrow her, like ye can borrow me for a brother.'

They walked on through the twilight.

'What "fi-ting", Fin?'

Ironically, it was a word she didn't know. Fighting was something McLennan did. It was not something he gave a name to.

'Fighting? I'll show ye!'

Fin broke away and launched into an energetic pantomime. First he pulled back an imaginary bowstring and fired an arrow, accompanied by a sharp whistling sound, followed its flight with eyes and pointing finger, and then played the victim, clutching his chest and falling over backwards. Then he jumped up and hurled a spear. Next he drew a sword and showed her a bout with much thrust and parry, dancing about on the turf.

Peony watched.

'Fin go fi-ting?'

'Naw, no' me, I'm no' old enough. But Donald might have to, and maybe Malcolm, and Father.'

'Don-al want fi-ting?'

Fin laughed. 'It's naught to do wi' us wanting or no' wanting. The Master's will is the law, and it's his quarrel that we have to fight in.'

'Why?'

'That's the way it is. Because we've all got liege-lairds. Our master too, he's got a laird above him. Only the King hasna. We all owe allegiance to them that's above us, and have to fight for our lairds. If we dunna, we'll lose our land and our livings and if another laird, or maybe the English some day, come to attack us, our laird wullna protect us. Ye canna live wi'out a laird.'

They walked on. Then Peony, who was frowning, asked,

'Ma-kri-nan go fi-ting?' Fin nodded strongly. 'Why fi-ting? Fi-ting make dead. Fi-ting no good.'

'Och, well, but it's what they do when there's a quarrel.'

'Kwa-rel?'

'Aye. Ye know. When people are angry wi' each other, they quarrel.'

'Why Ma-kri-nan angry?'

'Let's walk on, and I'll tell ye. But it's no' a nice story, so be prepared.'

They walked on through the twilight, the heather rough on their bare ankles.

'Ye see,' Fin began, 'a long time ago there was a quarrel between the Master and another laird, McInnes. One of his – McInnes's, I mean – got killed in a fight. I think it was his kin. After that McInnes sent men to make a raid on the Master's home. He didna live in a castle then, he just had a gie big house. They tied the Master up and stole his wife and killed his wee'uns.'

He had to say it all twice, but suddenly, like a blow to the heart, Peony understood. She understood so much that she couldn't bear the knowing of it – she felt as if she might break apart from understanding it.

She stopped in her tracks. Fin tramped on a few steps,

then turned and looked back at her, startled. Her eyes were black with shock and her free hand had dropped her skirt and flown to her mouth as if to hold back vomit, or a cry. She stood like that for a full minute, tense and shaking, then crouched down to the ground, and began to weep.

'Wee Eyes – I mean – Little Flower – don't – what's wrong?' He crouched, too, putting his arm around her, trying to look into her averted face. 'It's just a thing that happened. It was bad aw'richt, but it's over now.'

She shook her head.

'Not over. Never. Not over.'

Chapter Nine

九

McLennan determined the best time for the raid he planned on his enemy. It would be a moonless night in the month of May when there was good hope of fair weather. Well in advance, he sent out riders to summon a hundred of his strongest men. Some came willingly, eager for a change and a challenge. Others, like Fin's brother Donald, came reluctantly. Donald's bent was farming, not fighting. He had no wish to leave his home and risk his life, but there was no choice.

McLennan kept them quartered in the village for a couple of days while he put his carpenters to work on an exact copy of the catapult-on-wheels he had seen in Chi-na. It was to be made in pieces that could be assembled later. He got his masons to fashion big balls of stone and made arrangements to have them dragged on hurdles by strong horses. When that was done, he gathered his fighting men into the inner ward of the castle and rallied them.

'No doubt ye ken well why I've called ye and where we're going,' he shouted. 'I've a score to settle. A wrong done me is a wrong done to every last man of you. Ready your weapons,' he told them. 'We leave at dawn tomorrow.'

They did as he ordered.

Donald spent the night in the stable with Fin. They talked about the raid to come. Fin was in a state of high excitement. Before Donald could grumble much, Fin's enthusiasm began to infect him, so that he remembered his duty to his laird and put aside his reluctance.

'I came in place of Father,' he boasted, not quite truthfully – the recruiting officer, seeing the two of them together, had picked Donald. 'He's too old now and Mother needs him. Did ye know that in six months we're to have another wee brother or sister?' But Fin wasn't much interested in that. All he could think about was the coming battle and how Donald might bring honour on the family with brave deeds. Whatever he might think of the laird personally, it was a privilege to fight for him in a good cause, and a man might win gold and favours if he stood out in courage or devotion.

'I wish I could come! I'd show that black-hearted murderer!'
Fin kept saying.

*

McLennan chose his best horse, his sharpest sword and his
heaviest club. At dawn, his men, willing and unwilling
alike, ranged before him in the shadowed ward. In the dull
dawn light, he inspected them and their weapons. They all
had their bows and arrows, and some had swords and pikes,
as well as *dhus*. Then, because these were freeborn Scots
who would fight better when they understood their orders,
he told them his plan. It was a good plan, but it depended
for success on the element of surprise.

The castle gate was opened, and the drawbridge lowered.
McLennan was just going to ride across the moat. But
something was wrong. Something was missing.

'Where's the girl?' he roared suddenly. 'I want the
girl!'

The men from outside the castle didn't know what he
was talking about. All except one. Donald knew. Peony was
in the stables with his brother – Donald had just said
goodbye to her and claimed a kiss for good luck. 'Since I
havna a sister, you must do the office!' Its shy feather-touch
was still tingling on his cheek.

But such were the ingrained habits of blind obedience to the laird, a slavish desire to please him, that he didn't let himself stop to think. He ran in there, picked her up with not a word said, and carried her into the ward.

Fin, who had been tending a horse, let out a howl. But before he could move or utter again, a heavy hand fell on him and another stifled his mouth. He struggled, but Rob had three times his strength and pinned him to the stable wall, his eyes fierce and compelling.

Out in the yard, McLennan's brow cleared. 'Ah! Good. Put her up behind me.'

Donald obeyed, Fin's cut-off shout of protest ringing in his ears. Then he turned shamefacedly and went back into the ranks. Every man present avoided his eyes, because they all had the same thought. Take a wee girl into danger? It was cruel. It was needless. But they dared not say anything. The laird's will was law – their only law.

Peony, trembling all over with shock, struggled to pull out her skirt, which was hampering her legs. Once again, she locked her arms around her master's waist and hid her eyes against his back, holding her breath and clenching her teeth.

Fin had wrenched free of Rob with an eel-like squirm, and run out after her. He was trembling, too. He stood in the stable doorway with Rob's hand hard on his shoulder, holding him tightly, restraining him.

'There's naught to be done, lad, naught to be done,' he muttered over and over in a husky undertone.

The raiding party crossed over the drawbridge, which was pulled up behind them, and down the ramp. The portcullis crashed down with a sound of absolute finality.

The moment Rob released him, Fin ran up the stone stairs on to the battlements and watched them marching away, with McLennan at their head. He could see Peony clinging on behind. He felt the useless anger inside him, like a huge lump stuck behind his breastbone. Tears blurred the scene.

'I may never see her again,' was his thought, and it brought desolation. 'Puir lassie. Puir wee thing. She'll be so afeared! How can a man be so hard, and still call himself a man? If I'd a bow I'd shoot him dead from his horse this instant. I'd get over the moat somehow, I'd run and fetch her back. I'd make her safe.'

But none of that was going to happen, and he knew it even as the power of the wish was possessing his whole being. It made the wish as heavy as a stone in his brain, weighting him down, making it hard to move or breathe as he watched the raiding party grow smaller with distance – through the slumbering village, and out across the moor.

*

McLennan marched his men for two days, reaching his goal – an oak and beech wood two miles from the enemy castle – on the afternoon of the second. There were to be no fires. The men were soon huddled up in their plaids and sheepskins, looking forlorn and hungry. They had reached the wood too late to hunt, but McLennan, mindful of keeping their loyalty, heartened them as well as he could.

'The wood's full of deer, squirrels, pheasants... ye'll no' go hungry after tonight. Sleep, and your bellies will sleep and no' trouble ye.'

There was a subdued murmur among the younger men, but they obeyed. Donald rolled himself up in his plaid between thick roots that snaked around the base of an ancient beech. He sighed and shivered, wishing himself at home in his warm bed. He had a guilty conscience, too. Fin's face when he had picked up the lass... No. It did no good to keep yourself awake with such troublesome thoughts. He'd only been obeying orders. If he hadn't fetched her, someone else would have done, and got the credit for it, too. He hoped

Fin wouldn't tell their mother, though. Oldest son or not, Donald still feared his mother's anger, and she would be angry at this.

McLennan himself, after seeing his force encamped under the trees, lowered Peony to the ground without a word, and rode through to the far side of the forest. From there, sheltered by the outermost fringe of trees, he could see his enemy's castle on a rise, silhouetted against the last of the light.

'It's no' as big as mine!' thought Bruce McLennan. 'It's crude, next to mine, not more than a fortified mansion. One tower – no moat and no drawbridge.'

Still, its castellated walls and gatehouse looked formidable, and on that single tower he could see a watchman patrolling back and forth... Storming it would not be easy. But McLennan had his plan. After surveying his intended prize for an hour, marking every strategic point until darkness hid the scene, he rode back to the camp.

On his return, the first thing he did was to scan the sleeping company for Peony. It was hard to see her in the deep darkness under the trees that did not even admit starlight. But she came to him. She had food for him and had spread a blanket in a fairly comfortable place. 'No tea,' she said, smiling up at him. 'No fire.'

'Be quiet. Dunna wake the men. Bring water from the stream for my horse and for me.'

She struggled back from the stream with a leather pail full of water. Then she curled up as near him as she dared. She watched him covertly as he lay on his side, eating and drinking. She didn't sleep until he did.

*

The raiding party, hidden by the wood, spent two days assembling the siege-engine and practising with it. McLennan had thought of an improvement over the Mi-Ki version. He had had his blacksmith construct a special, shovel-shaped iron piece to top the throwing-arm. He now instructed some men to encase several of the heavy stone balls in bent branches. Between stone and wood they stuffed sheep's wool smeared with pitch. The pitch would be set alight, and the flaming balls flung over the enemy's walls by the giant catapult.

They cut down a tough young oak and shaped its trunk into a battering ram to break down the gates. They also made ladders out of branches to scale the walls.

McLennan had picked a small group to hunt. The hunters duly shot some birds, squirrels and rabbits, but saw no deer. It wasn't enough, and McLennan knew they wouldn't fight well with empty bellies. So on the second morning, before dawn, he took a gamble, which seemed reasonable at the time. He sent a small raiding-party to steal sheep from one of the farms around the castle. He warned them to be stealthy, and to steal at most two or three animals so that they wouldn't be missed.

At noon that day, looking at the progress that had been made, McLennan was satisfied. When he saw the three stolen sheep being brought in and skinned, he turned his mind to the problem of cooking them.

'How can meat be cooked without making smoke?' he asked one of his older men.

'By digging pits, m'laird.'

McLennan ordered other work suspended while three pits were dug, and dead wood collected. The fire was kindled in the pits, and smoke was wafted in all directions by men fanning it with leafy branches so that it kept close to the ground till most of it was dispersed. Next, large stones and green branches were laid on the glowing wood to stifle the flames and hold the fire in the embers. The carcasses were wrapped each in a rush mat soaked with water, and some of the earth was then piled loosely on top. What emerged was steam, and after some hours, an aroma of cooking mutton that brought saliva to every mouth.

That night they unearthed the meat and rent it to pieces between them with lusty shouts. But even while they laughed and guzzled, gnawing on the bones and feeling an unusual warmth toward their master, the farmer they'd robbed was on his way to the enemy castle to report his loss to his laird.

*

Archibald McInnes, although a man of savage instincts and a drunkard, was no fool. He had been waiting for something like this from McLennan for many years. The news about the missing sheep – though a man with less on his conscience might have thought it meant nothing – made his veins run ice.

He sent out spies.

They tracked the thieves, and came back with the news that there was a big party of men in the woods, with weapons including a siege-engine. McInnes broke out in a sweat, put away his whiskey and got ready to defend himself.

He sent runners and riders out into his lands according to custom, and ordered all his men who could fight, and their families, inside his walls. He urged the utmost speed and stealth, with threats that galvanised them all. The men frenziedly prepared their arrows and the women drew up tubfuls of water out of the well. They built their own fires ready to be lit on the edges of the roof, and carried up pots of water.

While these preparations were in progress, McInnes remembered he was a Christian and sent for a priest to shrive him of his sins. But there was one cardinal sin he was afraid to confess, a sin ten years old. A sin for which he assumed that no forgiveness was possible.

*

McLennan sat among his men, ate moderately and reviewed his plan. Peony, at his side, was given titbits almost from his own mouth, he was so certain of success. Soon he would have his just revenge. Soon his enemy would be dragged back in chains at his horse's tail and locked in his dungeon at his mercy.

The day after the feast was the last before the planned attack. McLennan moved among his men from dawn till dusk, making sure everything was ready for the march which was to begin two hours before midnight. They would have to march *around* the wood. They couldn't drag the great catapult through it.

When all was ready, and the men asleep, McLennan, too, decided that, after all, a prayer would be a wise precaution. His words to God were as terse as to his fellow men. He knelt on the ground some distance from his troops and gave his order to the deity.

'God give me the victory I deserve over my cursed enemy.'

He rose to his feet. This seemed a little abrupt, even to him, though at least no word of reproach had crossed his lips. After hesitating, he knelt down again.

'And forgive me my sins.'

But he was confident that no wrong he had ever done compared with the one done him, that he was about to avenge.

For the remaining hours until it was time, McLennan sat on in the dark under a tree and withdrew into himself. Regarding the coming raid, everything that needed to be thought about had been; all that needed doing was done. What he must do now was to rouse in himself the utmost courage, ferocity and determination. It was time to look again at the thing he had pushed down into the bottom of his memory and tried to bury because of the pain it gave. Now pain could be a goad.

Quite deliberately – and this took immense courage – he recalled the last moments in the life of his family. The memories he always fought, he now summoned. He saw the face of a bonny young woman, a face too much loved and mourned to be remembered clearly, screaming long, fierce screams as she was thrown across a man's back, her hand reaching out to him, fingers spread... He could hear the cries of children, cries cut short one by one. He shifted his arms and legs in a spasm, his limbs remembering how they had been unable to move then against their bonds. He clenched his fists till his nails pierced his palms, and screwed up every muscle of his face in an effort to endure the memory. It seemed suddenly that it had been an act of cowardice and betrayal, all these years, to struggle to blot out those scenes, those sounds, just because they tortured him.

He visualised his wife being carried away. He saw again her face, and it was a mask – hardly the face he'd known and loved, whose eyes had been bequeathed to all his children, but a thing distorted with terror and outrage. He saw it so clearly – forcing himself – that his breathing became erratic and his hair stirred almost audibly on his head.

He turned the fearful eyes of memory on to his children. He must think of them, too, recall them in every detail.

Chapter Nine

Their sweet faces, their innocence, and the remembrance of their death-cries would surely put hellfire into his blood. So he called them up, one by one: two daughters and his little son, his heir that should have been...

But something happened in his mind.

Their faces would not come to him. Instead of their remembered faces, each of them had *the same face,* and when he saw whose it was, he froze with incredulity. It was the face of – of the girl, of his nameless Mi-Ki slave.

The shock was terrible.

He groaned, ground his teeth, pummelled his head with his fists to change the images, to bring his children's faces back. But it was no use. There she was, curse her – each one of their bodies bore her head – how dared it be so, but it was! Like some malevolent, ghostly thing that had taken them over, she occupied an unmerited, intruding place in his mind and memory, the place belonging to his children. As if she – that scrap of foreign waste that he had scooped up and bought for his use, like a pot or a blanket or a pair of boots – was daring to claim kinship with him. As if she were his own blood! *As if she had replaced his children!*

He rolled over on his side on the forest floor, clawing up handfuls of leaf mould. He crammed it over his eyes, rubbed it into his hair, into his beard. She had befouled his mind, stolen his memories, sucked at the source of his courage! That old woman in the cottage was right. The girl was a witch! He would have to rid himself of her.

But when at last it was time to get up, to steady and clean himself, to rouse his men, he had not thought how it could be done, and his mind, instead of being calm and clear, was as turbid as troubled waters.

*

At the darkest time of night, he ordered his men to wheel the siege-engine around the outer edge of the wood. It took six of them to drag it with ropes, three more to push from behind. Its wooden wheels and their rough-hewn axles squeaked and groaned each time it went over uneven ground. The men were uneasy and so was McLennan, riding alongside with Peony behind him. (Why had he taken her with him? Because he always took her. Because he didn't know how to leave her. Because he had not decided what to do with her.) He hadn't expected it to be so noisy. They would have to move it quickly up the hill and attack without delay, before the defenders were roused. Luckily the wind was in their faces, blowing the sounds away.

It was well after midnight when they reached the foot of

the hill on which McInnes's mansion stood. McLennan ordered complete silence, but he couldn't silence his horse. When a shrill whinny suddenly pierced the night, all the men felt a chill of fear. But they were still far enough away so that perhaps it hadn't been heard. McLennan ordered the pullers and pushers to be changed to fresh men and the siege-engine hauled up the hill as fast as possible, with the missiles being dragged behind on hurdles. He rode ahead of them at the trot. And abruptly reined to a stop.

He'd seen something that appalled him. All the men behind him stopped too. Those who were dragging the siege-engine braced themselves against its gravitational backward pull, and looked up for the first time, instead of at the ground. And they saw what he saw.

Between the crenellations around the building, sudden points of bright light sprang forth. Fires...! Those fires told McLennan at once that his enemy had been forewarned, that his purpose had been discovered.

He looked at the walls. He couldn't see the windows in the blackness, but he guessed that behind every one, a man with a bow and arrows was waiting in the dark. He knew what would happen when his men stormed the building that held his enemy.

McLennan's heart hammered and his limbs trembled, not with fear but with the most intense disappointment and frustration. The raid was doomed. There would be no conquest and no prisoners to take back and put in the dungeon. Once again his hated enemy would triumph. Unless...

McLennan's right hand reached slowly behind him. Peony was there, a soft, compliant figure... Suddenly he grasped her. He dragged her from behind him to the front. He held her on the pommel of his saddle and brought his mouth close to her ear.

'Listen to me,' he whispered. 'I know now why I brought ye. Ye're going to go up that hill. Ye'll walk around the building. Ye will cry and wail like a lost soul, just as loud as a body can wail! They'll think ye're a banshee. That'll put the fear of the devil into them.'

Peony partly understood. She understood what she had to do, and her heart froze. Alone in the dark of night, she had to walk up a hill and round that great black shape with its crown of fire, outlined against the stars. She had to cry and wail like a *banshee*.

She had heard the word. Fin liked to tell ghostly tales sometimes. She knew a banshee was something fearful. But she didn't know that it was a dread female spirit, that when a banshee wails around a building, those inside are filled with the fear of death. All she knew was that she was being asked the impossible.

She shook her head frantically. But McLennan didn't see or care. He lowered her to the ground. She stood there, helpless and terrified. He raised his whip.

'Do as I bid ye, afore I give ye something to wail about!' he muttered fiercely.

She clung to his leg, sobbing.

'I canna! I canna!'

She was begging him to have pity on her, not to demand this terrible thing of her. His answer was to bring the whip down. It cut her back right through her jerkin. She tried to cry out.

He reached down and blocked her mouth with his big hand. It gripped her whole face, lifting her off the ground.

'Not yet, ye simpleton! Wait till ye get up there, under the walls! Then feel your pain and cry for it, and for the pain I'll give ye if ye disobey my orders!'

*

Peony ran.

She ran away from her master and his small army of followers. Up the hill towards the castle, black against the stars. She kept her eyes on the small points of light in the embrasures at the top. They seemed to twinkle, to call her. She knew that was what she had to head for.

She had been ordered to cry and wail. She thought she could do it. She had always done as McLennan ordered, so surely she could do this. Her back hurt. Her heart hurt. She had enough sadness in her heart because of his harshness to cry and wail all night, and for many nights to come. Despite what she knew of her master, despite her new understanding, she had not expected this of him.

She limped to the top of the hill. The castle loomed above her. There was no moat – the walls rose out of the hilltop. She was panting, and stopped for a moment to catch her breath. Then, slowly and carefully, she began to walk beside the wall. She kept one small hand on the stones to guide her in the darkness.

The stones were very cold. She felt the coldness fill her hand, and creep up her arm. It seemed to reach her heart. Her heart stopped hurting. It felt frozen.

She thought, 'Now I must cry and wail. Now I must feel my hurt. Now I must let my hurt come out in a loud sound.' She opened her mouth and pushed out her breath, meaning to cry and wail.

Chapter Nine

But no sound came out. Not even a moan, let alone a cry that would frighten those inside the walls.

She struggled to cry out. She forced herself. But nothing came. All her life she had taught herself not to cry, not to groan, not to let out her pain, but to hold it inside her. Now that she needed to bring it out, she couldn't.

She walked on and on, touching the stones. She kept trying to obey her master's order. The muscles of her stomach clenched. Her mouth was wide open. It was as if she screamed *silently*. She thought of all the bad, sad, terrible things in her life: her mother binding her feet tighter and tighter, ignoring her sobs and pleas. The sudden devastating change when McLennan took her. The stench of blood and battle, the wounds, the squalor, the horrors she had seen as a young child. She thought of McLennan's harshness to her, his refusal to treat her as anything but a chattel. She thought of her back, where she could feel blood trickling down. But she *felt* none of it. None of it seemed real to her.

Instead, a very strange thing happened. It was the good things that came back to her. Her sisters who had loved and pitied her, their big, painless feet acting as her feet as they carried her on their backs. The kindness of Li-wu, and his wise words. The beautiful sights she had seen on the long journey along the Silk Road, the golden dawns over the desert, the snowy mountains turning pink at sunset, and then the green fields of the west. The moment when she brought McLennan tea on the ship, and he fell asleep, and she touched his red beard and felt the balm of forgiveness for him flowing gently over her, proving Li-wu was right, giving her something to live by. The old woman in the cottage, and Janet, Fin's mother — their warm arms, their affection, their motherly kindness. Her imaginary garden, created with such love — and so long neglected, because she hadn't needed to visit it since she'd found Fin.

And Fin. And Fin!

Li-wu had taught her too well. He had said, 'The sorrows of this life are a dream. Let only what is good touch your inner self.' He'd told her to seek nothing for herself. She had sought nothing, but she had found many little treasures of warmth and kindness. Little pleasures. Scraps of unexpected happiness, like the scraps of food that had somehow nourished her, inadequate though they were.

Peony wasn't able to cry because she couldn't feel any pain. She just walked on and on around the high, fortified walls until the battle started. By that time she was round the far side. She heard the shouts and cries; she heard the loud 'thock' of the monstrous sling-shot; she saw the reflection of the fireballs. She even thought she heard the faint whistle of arrows.

She sat down under the wall, with her back against the bulge at the base of it, and stared up at the stars.

She should have been terribly afraid, alone and desolate. But all she felt was peace.

Chapter Ten

McLennan had waited in the darkness to hear the 'banshee' begin to wail. When nothing happened, he flew into a blind fury. The hot blood he had aroused by confronting his memories boiled in his veins. He forgot good sense and strategy. He lost control of himself.

He stood up in his stirrups and shouted to his men, 'Attack! Attack!' Then he rode up the hill like a madman, yelling his battle cry.

His men followed, yelling like him. They were running toward certain defeat, and probably death, and every man of them knew it. But loyalty to their master carried them forward.

Those manning the siege-engine dragged and pushed it

up the hill. When they thought they had come within range, they stopped, but the siege-engine started to roll backwards. Those behind strained to hold it; those in front leaned into the ropes. But some had to let go, to find rocks in the darkness to put under its wheels, and there was an agonised cry from one of the pushers as one wheel rolled over him. The arrows from the castle were flying, burying themselves with multiple small thuds in the turf about ten yards ahead of them. They were only just out of bow-range.

Donald was one of the pullers. He saw a man running towards him through the gloom with a big stone, to act as a chock, in his hand. Abruptly he stopped, dropped the stone which slid down towards Donald, and fell forward, an arrow in his back. All Donald felt was hot relief that it wasn't him.

The rock stopped level with him. Still pulling on the rope, he twisted his body and gave it a mighty kick towards the back of the engine. Someone seized it and set it under the back of one wheel. The engine, rocking and unstable, slewed around – it seemed to those in charge of it that it had a will of its own, to retreat from the castle. It took long minutes filled with curses to get it straightened and to block the other wheel so it couldn't roll backwards.

Now that Donald could let go the rope, he was

responsible for lighting the fireballs with a tinderbox. While others twisted the thick ropes round the axletree by frantically turning levers on either side, Donald scraped feverishly with the flint. The dry grass in the box caught a spark, and Donald, panting with excitement, brought a twig ready dipped in pitch to the little flame, and transferred it to the fireball nestling in the 'cup' on the end of the catapult arm. The missile blazed up at once. When the fire had crept all around it, the signal was given to fire the catapult. As the tightly-wrapped ropes spun the axle, the arm snapped up, crashing to a stop against the padded crossbar. The missile, released, flew in a high, blazing arc towards the black shape of the brooding mansion with its bright crest of fires. The loud swish of the fireball through the air drowned out momentarily the sound of the killer arrows humming like hornets toward them in invisible waves.

But the siege-engine was on such a slope that the fireball landed short. It took long minutes to prepare the next, and while they did so, grim realisation seized them – they would have to move the engine forward, into arrow-range. Panting and shouting encouragement to each other, they heaved the engine up ten yards, losing two more men to arrows. Again Donald lit a ball while the rope was prepared, and this time the missile did fly far enough. They saw it land on the roof, behind the fires.

Donald and his crew raised a cheer before setting-to to prepare to fling another. They were all relishing the notion of their fireball causing chaos, setting fire to the enemy's stronghold. They didn't know that it had gone through the roof and landed in a flag-floored hall below, where the women rushed upon it. Water flung from a dozen pails put out the fire, leaving no more damage than a hole in the roof.

McLennan meanwhile waited till one salvo of arrows had landed, then made a dash for the wall. Jumping off his horse he shouted for a ladder. 'It's safe here, men! Get under the walls where the arrows canna touch ye!' Men with ladders came running. A flight of arrows struck the party and several fell wounded, but seeing the safe ground immediately below the battlements, others took up the task while the defenders were stringing their bows with new arrows. Ladders were put in place, and McLennan and several others started to climb.

At the same time the men with the heavy battering ram had brought it up to the heavily barred gate. As more and more men were hit by arrows, others took their places. The strongest men seized the battering ram and ran with it till it crashed into the gate with a shuddering jar that ran up their arms and across their chests, shaking their whole bodies. Then they backed off and ran at the gate again.

When they were right under the battlements, a sudden scream went up. Streams of boiling water from above were falling on them. Like scalded cats they fled, dropping the tree trunk.

McLennan did not get halfway up the wall before a rock dropped on him from above, striking his shoulder and knocking him off-balance. The ladder swayed and fell backwards. McLennan clung to it, his legs dangling. He fell feet first into a group of his men, who caught him safely and lowered him to the ground. Apart from his shoulder, which was badly bruised, he was not hurt.

But the shock of falling brought him to his senses. He knew he had made a terrible mistake in carrying out the attack. The battle was lost before it began. He needed his men. It was stupid to get too many of them killed.

He heard his horse whinny in the darkness. He staggered to it and mounted. In the first lull in the noise, he shouted, 'Back! Back! Fall back out of range!' Then he led the retreat down the hill, shouting the same words as he rode through his men.

They ran, dragging and carrying their wounded. The

siege-engine and the battering ram were left behind, along with a third of their number, dead or dying on the hill.

Fin's brother Donald lay sprawled beside the siege-engine, his tinderbox still in his hand. The small flame in it had ignited some dry tufts of grass on the ground beside him. The glow showed his young face with a look of surprise on it, and glistened up the shaft of the arrow through his heart.

★

Inside the walls, McInnes's commander reported, 'They're on the run, m'laird! Shall we give chase?'

'We'll give chase all right,' said the old man. 'But no' this night. I know the whereabouts of the man. Aye, I know that well enough! We'll give chase in our own good time.' And he went to his bed with a tankard of whiskey.

★

It wasn't till they were regrouping back in the wood that McLennan remembered Peony.

He stopped cold as if he had walked into a wall. Where was she? What had happened? Why hadn't she obeyed his order? He was used to Peony doing everything he told her. It didn't occur to him that he had finally given her an order she could not obey.

He had almost willed her death. If they'd seen her

coming and shot her, what of it? Or captured her? Why should he fear that? She could tell them nothing that mattered. *Leave her. Forget her. She has no importance. Leave her.*

These thoughts had not fully formed in his brain before he had wheeled his horse about and was raining kicks and blows on it to drive it through the forest. *So small – they'd no' ha' seen her coming – hiding somewhere, aye, that's it.* In the heat of battle she could not have come back to him. He must get to her before daylight came. That was all he knew.

His men, open-mouthed, watched him vanish through the trees. Then one muttered, awe-stricken, 'He's awa' back after the wee lassie!'

'First he risks her life, then his ain to save her,' said another.

'Aye. Maybe he'll be shot on the way,' said another.

They looked at each other, some fearfully, others with a grim smile. No one said 'Let's hope so!' – though they all dreaded his rage at coming back home beaten, and with no prisoner for his dungeon.

*

McLennan rode at full tilt back through the wood and round the bottom of the hill till he faced the back of the enemy stronghold. Then he tied his horse to a low branch and climbed the hill on foot. He was fearful that dawn would come and light the scene before he could find the girl and get away. He moved as quickly as he could for the injury to his shoulder.

He felt his anger growing inside him at having done what he had no intention of doing – no reason to do.

'She didna do as I bid her!' he thought. 'If she had, we might have beaten them!' By the time he reached the foot of the castle walls, he was sure it was chiefly Peony's fault that he had failed.

The back of the building faced east. The first streaks of dawn were making the horizon pale. By this faint light, he saw her, and his heart bounded in his chest. She was lying at the foot of the wall. Was she alive? *Was she alive?* He ran to her, saying in his head, 'They didna capture her! She's given naught away! That's what matters!' But what mattered was whether she was quick or dead.

He ran to her and crouched beside her. He touched her throat. Yes, her blood was beating there, he felt it in his fingers. The instant relief – like a white light in his own blood – that flooded him, he stifled in swift action.

He picked her up and put her across his shoulder, but the pain stabbed him. He cursed, and swung her on to his back, bending forward, holding her legs under his arms. He felt her hands fumbling at his neck. A strange gladness seized him. He began to run down the hill.

The light was getting stronger.

Halfway down, an arrow whistled past him. He jumped aside. He felt the girl on his back – her body was between him and the arrows, it would be hit first. A shield. Was this not good? Yet instinctively he twisted himself, exposing his left side to the arrows.

The next one struck him in the flesh of his arm.

He felt it as a powerful blow, as if he'd been hit hard by a stone, but looking down he actually saw the point come out – saw it come bursting through in a little spray of blood. He stared at it, incredulous. Then the pain started.

He cursed and ran on, doubled over, with blood running down his sleeve and more arrows falling round him. His brain was full of fury.

Anger always helped McLennan to be strong. Reaching the wood, he found his horse and threw Peony over the front of the saddle. Then he pressed his arm tightly against a tree to steady it, broke off the arrowhead where it came through his arm, and pulled the shaft out at the back, clenching his teeth against the agony. The shame of defeat – the futility of the battle and the slaughter, the loss of his men — and now, this. His left arm useless. Awful pain. It was all the girl's fault, all of it! She was a witch — she had brought this on him out of spite, to punish him! Why had he felt gladness to find her alive, why, when he'd wanted her dead, had he turned his body to protect her? Better she were dead, much better, than to let her twist his actions into their own opposites! Curse her, it might be thought that she mattered!

He climbed on his horse by standing on a fallen tree, and rode off at full gallop through the wood, shouting, 'Ye'll pay for this, ye wicked wee devil! I'll make ye pay!'

Chapter Eleven

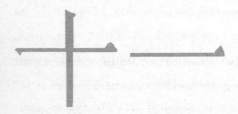

He caught up with his men. They noticed the girl, flung over the saddle. They saw her move and knew she was alive. Many of them had kind hearts, and were glad, but they looked at his face, frozen with hatred, and feared for her now, and for themselves, his unsuccessful raiders.

The raiding-party marched home in grim silence, McLennan riding at their head. They were silently mourning their dead friends and neighbours. They marched for two days, stopping only briefly to sleep and tend the wounded. McLennan allowed no time for hunting or eating. His mind was seething with poison. In the night he tied Peony to a tree and would not even give her water.

At midnight one of the older men dared to creep to her

on his belly to bring her a drink. They exchanged two whispered words.

'Do-nald?'

'Dead.'

She turned her face into the earth.

*

At sunset the following day, from the gatehouse casement Fin watched them coming, the sad procession. His eyes flew instantly to Peony, lying across the Master's saddle. 'She's dead!' he thought, and his heart seemed to shrivel up. He forgot to look for his brother, but ran down crying to Rob, 'She's dead!'

Rob said, 'She's no' dead, lad. He'd no' have bothered bringing her home if she was dead.' To himself, he muttered, 'Maybe better for her if she were.'

Fin was in the courtyard when they rode in. He dared not touch Peony until McLennan had dismounted, thrown him the reins, and stumbled away, clutching his arm. Then Fin lifted her tenderly down.

'Are ye aw'richt, Wee Eyes – Little Flower?' he whispered.

Exhausted and battered by the events of the past days, she still managed to nod and smile at him. His spirits took off like a bird.

'Och, but ye're a braw lassie!' he cried, and held her for a moment in his arms.

'See to the horse!' ordered Rob loudly, adding in an undertone, 'And gi' the lass something to eat and drink.' He, too, was mightily relieved to see Peony safely back. As the two children went into the stable close to each other, it was Rob who took the horse while scanning the motley, blood-stained, depleted crowd of men, noting with a sinking heart that the lad's brother was missing.

In the dim familiar stable, their place of refuge, Fin hugged Peony and settled her deep in some clean straw. She was shaking with cold and weariness, and now her back did hurt. He wrapped her in a horse-blanket, brought her water to drink and dug out a piece of rookie pie for her. She ate it ravenously.

'What happened to ye? Was it terrible? Did he go mad when he didna win?' he asked. And then suddenly, like a thunderstroke, he remembered. 'Where's Donald? Is he aw'richt?'

She looked at him wordlessly. His face, all one big smile a moment before, now fell into lines of alarm. 'Och, he's no' dead! Tell me he's no' dead!' he whispered pleadingly.

She closed her eyes against his look of suffering she knew

would come. He threw himself face down beside her and choked the tears back as he thought of his mother and the family table, now forever blighted with an empty chair. Peony watched him, and at last reached out and stroked his hair. His inner stiffness broke at her touch and he sobbed and let his tears flow.

*

McLennan had to have his wound seen to, before he could do the thing he meant to do, the thing he had decided on during the long march home. So Peony had a little time left.

She spent it with Fin in the stable, untroubled by any fear. McLennan had come back for her, he had carried her through the showers of deadly arrows and turned his body so that she wouldn't be hit. The fact that he had thrown her over his pommel instead of letting her ride behind him, that he hadn't spoken a single word to her and had not let her serve him nor sleep near him during the journey was a little disturbing, as was the tying – he had never done such a thing before. But she was used to his rages and moods; she knew that part of her duty to him was to absorb them. It never entered her head that he might blame her for his defeat, even though she had not been able to carry out her task.

She and Fin sat together, with the good warm smell of horses and hay around them, and she tried to tell him what had happened. He couldn't make much out of her tale.

'He told ye to wail and cry? What for?'

'Ban shee,' she said earnestly. But she said it in such a foreign way that he didn't recognise the word. 'Tell me in English, Wee Eyes!' But she couldn't explain. Still, she was able to tell him how she'd walked around the cold black walls at night, and how she'd thought of him and felt happy. He understood that all right.

'What a beast he is, to send ye off by yerself in the dark! Who can tell what got into his head! I wish I'd been with ye!' And he put his arm around her. 'But ye did it!'

She shook her head. She hadn't done it. She felt a slight shiver of unease because she hadn't done as she'd been told.

Fin didn't notice. He was so glad to be with her. He thought it a triumph that she had got to the castle all alone, and passed the night under its walls while the battle raged, and lived to come back to him. 'Ye're such a braw lass!' he said again and again. She didn't know what 'braw' meant, but she knew he was pleased with her. She leant against him and smiled and smiled. She felt again the warmth and comfort of being close to someone who cared for her. She felt the happiness she'd felt in the cottage with the old woman. Only this was better. This was *the* happiness, like being in her garden, only it was real.

*

McLennan came looking for her at sunset.

He had had his arm bound up. The doctor-barber who did it was clumsy; his fingers were blunt and rough, and he had hurt him. He had cursed the man roundly, shouting at him to get back to his haircutting, wanting Peony with her small, gentle hands. But he gritted his teeth and wouldn't let himself send for her. He sensed that if she tended his wound, he would lose the will to punish her.

And he had to punish her. Someone had to suffer for what had happened to him. And for what might happen. Because he had begun to look ahead. McInnes would hardly let matters rest as they were, even though – McLennan ground his teeth again at the thought – he had not lost a single man. Oh yes. Someone must pay for this! The witch must pay!

He stood in the stable doorway. Fin and Peony looked up when his shadow fell on them. Peony jumped to her feet. She wasn't afraid, she was concerned for him when she saw the wrapping on his arm. She even ran to him and looked up into his face, eagerly, because he had come looking for her and might need her, which would mean his bad mood had passed.

But what she saw in his eyes suddenly struck fear into her very marrow. She backed away – Fin was on his feet too – and shrank against him, and Fin, seeing the black hatred in the Master's face, tried to get between them. But it was no use.

Bruce McLennan strode up to them. He knocked Fin out of the way, sending him flying against one of the wooden stable partitions. He picked Peony up and carried her out into the courtyard.

Fin got up. His head was muzzy from where McLennan had clouted it. He stumbled out into the ward. He saw McLennan with Peony under his good arm, disappearing into the darkness of the castle. There were no battlements, no moat now, to stop him running to rescue her. But his legs wouldn't obey him.

He stood motionless, powerless, with the most horrible foreboding in his heart.

*

Bruce McLennan carried Peony down a long flight of stone steps. At the bottom was a flaming torch, set against the wall in a metal basket. It showed a great door with iron hinges and nails with large round heads driven into the wood. It had a lock with a keyhole as big as an eye on edge... McLennan put Peony down.

'Dunna move or I'll kill ye,' he said.

She didn't believe it. Though almost fainting from fear of him now, she still thought it was an empty threat. But she had a flashing memory of how she had pleaded with him not to send her up the hill in the dark. She remembered what she had not let herself remember, the cruel cut he had given her with his whip. He had done that when she'd been begging him. What would he do to her now?

He took a huge brass key from his belt. He put it in the lock and turned it. It made a terrible screeching sound. The door swung open.

Inside was only darkness.

McLennan pushed Peony in. She resisted. Her resistance angered him more. He thrust her into the dungeon so hard that she fell on her knees on the wet stones. Then he stood in the doorway.

Peony crouched on bruised hands and knees for a few moments, and then slowly knelt up and turned. She saw only his familiar black outline against the flaming torch. She could see his wild hair trembling on his head, and his chest heaving. She couldn't believe what was happening.

'I'll no' chain ye,' said this fearsome black figure. 'A witch should be chained. But ye've served me, so I'll no' chain ye. But I'll no' let ye out.' He paused, as if waiting for someone to stop him, but there was nothing but silence and her white face against blackness. He knew he should stop talking now, finish the thing, and go. But somehow he went on speaking, not letting himself see it as a kind of argument.

'It's no' just that ye disobeyed me. Ye put a curse on my enterprise, or I'd no' have failed. Ye're a witch and ye dunna deserve to live. Think yourself lucky I dunna burn ye.'

He took the key out of the lock and held it up.

'Ye see this key?' he said. 'It's going in the river this hour. Ye'll never see the light of day again! And so perish all who go against their laird!'

And he backed away and swung the great door shut.

But not quite quickly enough to prevent himself hearing her voice, a voice that, because of her quiet ways, he seldom heard, suddenly piercing and as Scots as his own.

'Och, dunna! Dunna! Dunna!'

As his children had cried! The same plea! Oh, she *was* a witch, or how could she know to plead just as they had?

His hand made to turn the key back without his order. For a long, long moment he stood there, gripping it with whitened knuckles. Two men warred in his breast, the father who had helplessly heard his children's last cries, and the man of wrath, bent on vengeance. Then, with a terrible effort, he wrenched the great brass key from its lodging and ran up the steps as if pursued by demons, leaving the torch to burn itself out.

*

Peony heard the screech of the key turning in the lock. She froze with horror. He was leaving her. It was not just an angry threat. Those were his heavy, running footsteps on the stone stairs. She watched in dawning realisation as the strip of torchlight under the door got dimmer and dimmer, and then vanished.

She saw, as clearly as if it were before her, the key flying out from his hand over the battlements and down into the river. In that awful darkness she could see nothing real, but she seemed to see the key, landing with a splash, sinking into the water, lying on the muddy bottom. Never to be found. Never able to let her out.

She believed he would do it. Now she truly believed it. And, believing it, her inner world collapsed.

She had never really thought him evil. Harsh, yes. Ill-natured, yes. Cruel — sometimes, when he was hard-pressed, when his rage got the better of him. But who that knew of his suffering could blame him for his black moods? She hadn't blamed him, even before she knew. He was a young soul. He couldn't help himself.

But this?

Her vision of the drowned key at once took away any hope she might have had that he would change his mind. Even if he did, he couldn't let her out without the key.

Chapter Twelve

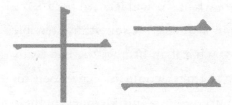

Bruce McLennan climbed directly from the dungeon up on to the battlements and leaned out between two blocks of stone. He drew back his hand with the key in it and commanded himself to throw it.

He could imagine it flying, fatally, unrecoverably, down into the murky water. That would settle it. That would fulfil his given word.

But his hand would not obey him. His fingers gripped the brass loop at the top of the key in a rigid grip and would not let go.

McLennan stood poised between good and evil, between mercy and vengeance.

At last he came to himself a little. The raw edge of his

anger blew away in the gusts of wind from the moor. He had not meant what he'd said. Of course he was not going to let her die down there. He'd threatened it to frighten her, to punish her, to show her who was master. But he would let her out after a day or two, when she had learned her lesson.

He lowered his arm in a spasm, for something terrible had almost come to pass. What if, in his rage, he had really flung away the key? How, then, would he have used his dungeon for its avowed purpose – to shut McInnes up there some day, and bend him to his will? Hah! He needed his dungeon! No, certainly the key must be kept, and kept safe. He strung it to his belt and descended the steps again to begin planning his defence.

*

McLennan's first duty now was to summon within his walls all vulnerable tenants, and house them there until the danger had passed. There were now a lot of these defenceless people – orphans and widows whose men had died in the failed attack. He owed them protection, and maintenance; with a counterattack expected, he must send armed men out to escort them to safety. He must garrison the village.

A laird who had inherited his position from his forebears

would have done it immediately, so deeply ingrained was the concept of *noblesse oblige*, the responsibility of the highborn for the low who served them. But McLennan was a come-lately laird, son of common folk. His considerations were practical; his first priority was survival, his second, revenge.

First came the defence of his castle. How could he conduct its defence when it was cluttered with women and children that he had to feed?

When he had spent five or six hours alone, planning strategy, he came to a hard decision that was going to have terrible consequences. He had only a limited number of messengers and armed escorts at his disposal, and he needed to let his fighting men know what he required of them. So he would bring in only the people he needed. The rest would have to take their chances. He had more important considerations.

*

'But where is she? Where's he taken her?'

Fin stood in front of Rob, desperately blocking his way. The groom took the boy by the shoulders, but then, looking into the eyes he'd been trying to avoid, he dropped his head with a heavy sigh.

'My lad, ye must forget her.'

'*Forget her!*'

'Aye. For she's where Donald is, or as near as makes no odds.'

The boy stiffened and turned ashy white. 'Ye don't mean – he's killed her!'

'He's locked her up.'

'That's not being dead! He'll let her out! Ye said she was his candle! He'll no' be left alone in the dark!' Fin was gasping now, for it was a real dark he was thinking of, the lassie's dark, locked in the dungeon. Already it was twenty-four hours since the master had borne her away from the stable.

'Listen, Fin. It's full moon tomorrow. Ye need to gang hame to see your mother.'

'Tell her, ye mean,' said Fin fiercely. 'I've to tell her – about Donald.'

'Aye, and then give her comfort.'

Comfort? What comfort was there? Donald killed, and now Little Flower – his own Wee Eyes – locked away in the depths of the earth, as stone-stifled as if already in a tomb. Where was the comfort to be got or given?

Rob saw his distress. But he had no more time to give him. There was work to be done. He had to ride out and bring orders to the far-flung tenants. Very strange orders, to his thinking, but it was not his way to think too much.

'Get Cora ready,' he said shortly, naming a fast mare.

Fin straightened. His eyes were red, his jaw tight. 'I wullna.'

'Ye what?' asked the groom in astonishment.

'I'll no' serve him. Not now.'

Looking into his furious face, Rob suddenly feared for him, for his youth and passion and recklessness. He did what he felt he had to, to save the boy from dangerous folly.

Raising his voice suddenly, he roared, 'Do as ye're bid!' Fin jumped, and then felt a stinging slap to his cheek that knocked him sideways. Before he could stop his head ringing, he was grasped and thrust forcefully towards the mare's stall. Shocked and dizzy, he got her ready. The habit of obedience was stronger than rebellion.

Rob said no more, but prepared to ride out on his mission. At thirteen Fin should already have learned that self-control, loyalty and obedience alone spelled survival in the feudal world. If he hadn't, it was Rob's place to teach him.

But his hand still held the sting of the blow it had given, and at the last minute he relented.

'Work done?' he asked gruffly, when he was already

mounted in the courtyard. Fin nodded sullenly. 'Jump on behind then. I'll take ye home. I've to go there anyhow.'

*

All the way home Fin tried to prepare himself for telling his mother and father they'd lost their eldest son. But when he got there, he didn't have to do it. Word had already reached them and the house was in mourning.

Rob tethered the horse and together they went in. Janet was sitting by the fire with her shawl over her head, crying in groans, with Jamie, pale and stunned, close at her side. No one else was there. When she saw Fin she threw her arms out for him to come to her. He had nothing to do but be hugged and share her misery.

'Och, Donald!' she wailed, clinging to Fin as if she were drowning. 'My dearie! My darling boy! Dear God, why did Ye take my beautiful son?'

Fin cried for his mother. It broke his heart to see her so wretched, and the pain pushed Peony for a little while to the back of his thoughts. Rob stood awkwardly, turning his bonnet in his big hands, looking at the ground. At last Janet noticed him.

'This is Rob, Mother.'

Janet rose unsteadily. 'Aye – I've heard good things of ye,' she said, her breath ragged. 'Ye've been good to Fin.' Rob, thinking how he had slapped him, flushed and didn't meet her eye, but said, 'I'm gie sorry for your loss.'

'Thank ye. What have ye come for?'

'To see your man.'

'He'll be back soon.'

The four of them sat in silence till the head of the house returned from work. He, too, had red eyes and when he saw Fin he brushed them with the back of his hand. He hugged the boy tightly, then acknowledged Rob.

'You bring orders from the laird?'

'Aye.'

'McInnes will counterattack?'

'Aye, it's expected.'

'So we're all to get inside the castle walls with our women and wee'uns.'

Rob shuffled his feet. 'No. That's no' it.'

'What? But in time of war—'

'The laird's plan is to have some men within to mount a frontal defence. That will include you and your – your sons. He wants other men to muster under commanders he'll send, to go around behind McInnes's force and attack them from the rear.'

'Just me and my big lads are to go? No' my wife?'

Rob nodded.

'And while we're away from home on the laird's business, who's to protect ma wumman and ma wee boy there? Are they to be left defenceless?'

Rob said, 'I've no orders as to that. Perhaps ye can leave young Angus at home.'

'Angus!' cried Janet. 'Of course he'll no' go! He's only fifteen!'

'There'll be younger than him under arms in this fight,' said Rob.

The father narrowed his eyes. It was not right. It was not according to custom. It did nothing to strengthen his loyalty to the laird, or the will to fight in his cause.

Still, there was no choice. Fight they must, himself, Malcolm, and Rab. What if one of them—? He glanced at his wife, who was gazing at him piteously, pressing both hands to her belly as if she could protect the baby growing there. The man's heart twisted. Surely a man's first duty was to his family! But it was not so. His first duty was to his liege-laird. Even a laird was subject to the law.

Except that this one seemed to think he wasn't. But Fin's father suddenly straightened his back and showed his teeth. If his laird could be canny and ruthless, so could he. He would march to the castle as ordered with his two older sons beside him – and his pregnant wife and younger sons at his heels. Let the laird turn them back if he dared.

*

Now all was activity and preparation, inside the castle and throughout the laird's lands and tenantries.

Those summoned to defend the castle mustered there, and many had had the same idea as Fin's father. They brought their families with them. McLennan, watching the little motley groups approaching the castle from three sides and crowding across the drawbridge, scowled furiously, for indeed he lacked the face to take in the men and reject the women and children. But perhaps it was for the best. No doubt the men would fight better to defend their families who were with them. The men left outside to make the surprise assault would fight like wild boars to keep the enemy from attacking their homes. A good strategy, surely.

The castle filled up with people. The men had to begin preparing its defences. The women and children had to settle in as best they could. Soon, they would have duties, too.

Fin, who knew every nook and cranny, led his mother and Jamie to the hayloft above the stables, a good warm private place, and helped settle them there. He felt fiercely glad that the grim walls stood between them and danger. And so did his father, preparing arrows and receiving orders in the ward, but he also had a thought to spare for those who'd been ordered to stay outside. This wild man, McInnes, had a reputation that was almost a legend. If the man had not scrupled to murder the laird's children and carry off his wife (who had died, it was said, of grief and shame), what might he do to theirs, left unprotected when their men had to go and fight?

*

As soon as he could, Fin ran to the kitchen to find food for his mother. The kitchen servants were frantically working to feed ten times their usual number.

'Have ye seen Wee Eyes?' he blurted out as he burst in.

'Wee Eyes, indeed!' muttered the cook, who, for Peony's foreignness, had always suspected her of spell-making. 'She'll no' be souring the milk and burning the meat nae more!'

Fin turned white. 'What d'ye mean?' he gasped.

Others gave him fearful looks. 'Dunna ask!' one

whispered, and nodded her head at the floor. 'She's—'

'Ye mean he's no' let her out? Two whole days – nearly three—'

'Hush, Fin! Hush! She's no' to be spoke of!' said another under her breath. 'Do ye no' know, she's a witch?'

Fin stared at her, winded by the hugeness of this lie.

'Didna I always say so?' called the cook, almost in triumph, looking like a fat goblin herself in the glow of the fire and a cloud of steam. 'Such a queer thing as she was, no' like a natural lassie! Besides, otherwise the Master'd never have locked her up, her that was his wee pet, and be stridin' about without shame, wi' the key hung from his belt. The spell she had him under must have broke, and he saw her clear for what she was!'

When hope is gone, Li-wu had once told Peony, there is only patience left.

She had patience. She had learned it. She sat quietly on the stone floor for hours, her eyes closed, trying to keep Li-wu's words vital and meaningful.

'*We pass through this world many times. This hard life will pass. You will have others. In one of them perhaps you will reach Nirvana, where one is free of desires.*'

But she had not reached Nirvana yet. She knew it because she had desires. She desired to live. She desired — longed, passionately — to see the daylight, to breathe freely, to eat, to drink, to stay alive and to be with Fin.

If Li-wu was right, these longings were for things as unimportant as dreams. She would pass through this world again. Next time would be better, if she could accept her fate this time. She must be resigned. The worst that could happen to her had surely happened. The hunger and thirst were not very much worse than she had often felt before. The cold and darkness, too, she might endure. And death? Just a door to something better.

But there was one truly cruel thing, one unbearable thing. It was her master who had put her here to die alone in the darkness. He had heartlessly abandoned her. Not only did he care nothing for her, but now she must face the fact that perhaps he was not just a damaged man, but a bad one. For the first time, it crept into her mind that she, a poor, humble slave-girl, was worth something better than to have wasted herself serving him.

This awful thought saddened her so terribly, it weakened her resolve to accept her fate in the spirit of Lord Buddha.

*

The attack came on the fourth day after McLennan had shut Peony in the dungeon. In all that time he had not thought of her because his mind was completely occupied by the coming struggle.

He was fairly confident of his plan. But he had reckoned without McInnes's low cunning and ruthlessness.

McInnes was a man without honour and without scruples. His strategy was to win at any cost. He had learned from McLennan's failure. He did not muster in a wood where spies could warn of his approach, or come marching up the hill in the dark of night, dragging a clumsy siege-engine. He didn't march on the castle at all, at first. He had other work to do.

*

The lookouts posted on the castle battlements ran down, white-faced, to report that columns of smoke were rising from farmsteads near and far.

An almost audible tremor seemed to pass over the people gathered in the castle. Men defied orders to rush up the steps to the top of the walls nearest to their own homes. Many were too distant to be seen, even from this height, but the men knew precisely which column of smoke showed that their particular house was afire. They leaned out as if they could reach their burning homesteads and put out the flames that were destroying them and their hard-won crops. But at least their families were safe! Each man sent up a prayer of gratitude for that. Then they descended, full of grim determination to be avenged when the enemy came within reach.

But when, some hours later, it became clear that not only the empty farmsteads, but those of their neighbours, who'd been left outside to fight, were being torched, a stifled outcry arose. McLennan was above on the battlements, and when he saw what was happening across the countryside, and sensed the mood in the castle below him, he felt seriously alarmed. He knew he had done wrong in leaving those families outside for his own strategic purposes, and he knew that the men he was counting on to fight for him could rebel, and would be within their rights if they did.

But luckily for him, rebellion was not foremost in their hearts. Foremost was retribution against the villain McInnes who had made such a cowardly attack on undefended homesteads, full of women and children.

★

Meanwhile, the men outside the castle knew nothing of the tragedy that had overtaken their homes and loved ones.

Chapter Twelve

Mustered in hiding-places amid the crags, they stood with their commanders, stolidly prepared to fulfil their obligations to their liege-laird. And when the order came – a beacon, lit from the castle walls – they deployed according to plan. As McInnes's main force at last made its frontal attack through the village below the castle walls, they closed in swiftly behind them, meaning to drive them forward into the hail of arrows and missiles the castle defenders were poised to deliver.

From behind the wall of the main gatehouse, McLennan could see the whole pattern of the battle. He watched in some amazement as McInnes, in heavy armour, mounted on a charger, broke easily through the gate in the palisade wall of the village, and directed his men to set fire to houses there. He watched his own men, his secret weapon, a jagged fringe of heads, then bodies, then running legs, appear over the top of the hill behind the enemy and charge down on them. And then, with a bellow of dismay, he saw a number of smallish groups – no men of his, the enemy's men! – suddenly appear as if from nowhere and charge in on his men from the flanks. Why had his scouts not warned him? He didn't know that they had all fallen into McInnes's hands, and, suitably persuaded, had revealed all they knew of McLennan's plans.

The enemy, out of reach of the castle's arrows, turned on the attackers and drove them away. Many were killed or wounded. The survivors ran to take refuge in their farmhouses. And there they made the horrible discovery of McInnes's treachery.

*

McInnes now laid siege to the castle.

McLennan was frantic. What could he do? He could try to get a messenger through the lines to make his way to some neighbour, and beg for support to break the siege. But the nearest was seventy miles away, and why should he risk his own men to save McLennan? Still, it was their only hope. So, just before the ring was closed, in the dead of night McLennan ordered three horsemen out through the postern gate and down to the river along the steep walled path. They were ordered to swim the river on horseback and ride like the wind to this neighbour and promise anything if he would send reinforcements to the beleaguered castle.

*

McInnes closed the circle the next morning. He even brought up some boats — his own land bordered the same river, higher up — to prevent escape and any supplies reaching the castle that way. Then, calmly confident, he settled down to starve McLennan and his people out.

He had the nearby village in a stranglehold. He plundered it of food, and kept the able-bodied men penned up in the hall that had once been McLennan's house, except for those too old or feeble to resist or run off. He forced the women to cook for them and serve them in other ways. Any man who resisted was killed and his home burnt. Resistance soon stopped, but in the big timber-framed hall, the men seethed and plotted.

There was nothing McLennan and his people could do but wait. Nobody could get in or out of the castle. There was no battle yet, because neither side's weapons could reach the other. But now McInnes assembled three siege-engines, brazenly, in daylight and in full sight of the castle's defenders. To McLennan's fury and chagrin, all were based on his Chi-na model that had been abandoned after the failed attack — his own weapon was to be turned against him.

At night McInnes sent parties down into the moat-ditch to undermine the walls. They did this under cover of portable wooden sheds covered with animal skins so that when McLennan's defenders fired flaming arrows down at them, they didn't catch fire. The spoil from the diggings was heaped in an adjoining part of the big trench, for use later when they would attack the walls with siege-towers, battering rams and ladders.

Watching the progress of this work every morning from the battlements, McLennan knew it was only a matter of time before missiles would begin hurtling over the walls, perhaps before portions of the walls themselves began to collapse. McLennan knew McInnes would only make his assault when the castle's defenders were weakened with hunger, and that must come soon. With the overcrowding, food stocks couldn't last long. McLennan had laid in stores, of course, but not having expected the families, he had failed to lay in enough.

The enemy, meanwhile, was not going hungry. They had all the food they needed. In fact they took a delight in feasting in full view of the castle, carousing on stolen casks of ale and wine, building fires and roasting whole sheep, pigs and oxen taken from the farms. They would wave their cups towards the castle as if toasting those they'd robbed. They danced with the dead animals before they cooked them, shouting mocking thanks for the good food.

They did worse. They brought up their captives and displayed them. The men inside the castle walls watched helplessly as the womenfolk of their neighbours and the villagers were paraded or held up or abused in clear sight below them. They could hear their cries and pleas mingled with laughter and jeering. Some of the men, when drunk, would prance almost to within range of the castle's arrows, lift their kilts and show their nether parts as the ultimate taunt.

All this drove the defenders to an unbearable pitch of helpless fury. Many arrows were let fly from bows shaking in the hands of men too outraged to hold back. They willed the slender missiles on, only to see them burying themselves in the turf twenty feet from their nearest enemy. And that enemy would then dare each other to creep forward at night and recover the arrows for use later against those who had shot them. This waste infuriated McLennan, who said he would flog the next man who let fly an arrow until he ordered it.

And hunger as well as thwarted rage began to grind the vitals of the men, sharpening them like steel against stone.

*

Meanwhile, as the days went by, Fin was locked in misery. His thin body felt like a cage that held nothing but awful imaginings which exhausted him so that, when at last he lay down each night on his bed of straw, he slept as the dead sleep, dreamless and deep and held down as if under layers of stones by an unwillingness ever to waken to more terrible thoughts.

His mother, Janet, who saw him every day about the castle – he still had to look after the horses, though there was no use for them now – watched him getting paler and thinner and more silent until she thought she was watching him waste away. But she didn't guess what was in his mind or she would have been panic-stricken.

*

Peony couldn't tell how time passed. She had no way to measure the hours, the days and nights. She tried to be patient and desire nothing. In this dire moment, she remembered her garden.

Her imaginary garden! It had been left behind somehow. Since she'd known Fin, she hadn't needed to visit it. Her real world was too all-absorbing. Now, as her eyes groped endlessly in the dark for some hard shape to give her her bearings, she saw her garden in front of her more clearly than ever before. And it dismayed her.

Like a real garden that isn't visited or tended, it was sad. The paving-pebbles were covered with dead leaves. The pavilion was unpolished, dull and silent, deserted by its musicians and by its guardian spirits. The pond was scummy with weed and the graceful red and white carp were all gone – dead, no doubt, or taken by herons because she hadn't looked after them.

And when, dreading what she would see, she looked up at the roof-corners for her dragons, she found they were gone, too. They had always been so alive for her. Naturally, she thought desperately, they would have flown away when she didn't come to see and talk to them. So there was nothing now to keep the evil spirits away. They would find the straight way to her, despite the care she had taken to make all the paths crooked.

Sad and lonely place, neglected and deserted! Her dear guardian dragons no longer perched above, protecting and caring for her!

She wept at last. She wept bitterly and aloud. Now if she had been outside the enemy's walls, those inside might indeed have thought that a lost soul was circling, for she shrieked and wailed without restraint as she had never done in her whole life, even from the pain of her bound feet.

Suddenly she fell silent, and a moment later, she sat up. A rebel thought had invaded her. Perhaps Li-wu was wrong.

Perhaps this life was not just one of many. Perhaps McLennan was robbing her of the only life she would ever have.

Anger and fear washed over her and she was filled with violent feelings. She needed to take some action.

She felt around on the floor. She found a chip of loose stone. She felt its edges. They were sharp. She stood up, and put her hands on the walls in the pitch darkness. She found a large, smooth, upright stone.

She knew she was going to go against everything Li-wu had taught her. But she thought, 'I have been a good person, and this is what has come of it. I have a bad person in me, too. I'll let my badness visit me and perhaps it will help me.'

Blindly she scratched some characters with the sharp stone. They were not words of patience and acceptance. They were a threat. She hoped she wouldn't be punished for them in her next life, but she couldn't help herself.

When the characters that she couldn't see were on the wall, she didn't sink down again on to the floor. She walked instead around the inside of the dungeon, her empty left hand touching the walls. When she touched the wood of the door, she stopped and leant against it, willing it to melt and let her out, but it was solid as the very earth that surrounded the dungeon. It would never open for her – never! How much more must she bear? Was Lord Buddha never going to take pity and come for her?

She began to walk again, but suddenly she stopped. She needn't wait for Lord Buddha! She had command of her fate. She had the power of death. The sharp stone that had carved her epitaph was clutched in her right hand. Despite her hunger and weakness, that right hand was still strong and obedient enough to do what she told it to.

She drew herself up.

'*Wo shi mudan*,' she said steadily aloud into the engulfing dark. 'I am Peony.'

It was like saying goodbye to herself.

Chapter Thirteen

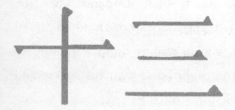

In the dead of night, McLennan, who had at last left the battlements and gone to his chamber to snatch some sleep, woke suddenly in the dark, his heart almost stopped in his breast. Someone was moving in his room.

The footsteps were light. He heard them on the stone floor. He heard some rustling, some unidentifiable movement. Then the steps were coming closer. He strained his eyes through the darkness. The slit window let in a strip of moonlight. A small shadow crossed it.

McLennan was not entirely free of superstition. He had the deaths of many people on his head. Fear flashed across his brain like fire. And then there was another flash, the flash of a knife blade.

Chapter Thirteen

McLennan's good arm shot up and as the blade came down, he grasped the hand that held it. He twisted it. There was a cry. This was no ghost! Gripping the thin arm, McLennan slid out between the silk sheets and dragged its owner into the moonlight.

It was the boy from the stable.

Once, McLennan would not have hesitated. He would have rammed his head against the stone wall and broken his neck.

But he couldn't. He lacked the strength and even the will to kill the intruder. Instead he dragged him out to the stables and woke the groom.

'This vixen's whelp tried to kill me,' he growled. 'Punish him. Punish him hard. Tell his father I'll hang the boy if he doesna control him.'

Rob, still half-asleep, could only gape at him. McLennan went back to his chamber with the reeling steps of a drunken man. Rob turned furiously on Fin. 'Are ye off your head? Attacking the Master?'

Fin looked wild. He said, 'He shut her up in that dark place. I have to get her out.'

'How can ye get her out, ye bauby? Now I must beat ye! Oh, curse ye, come outside so your mother won't hear!' And he took Fin out into the ward and beat him, but not harder than he had to, because he himself thought the laird guilty of an act of mortal wickedness. Fin felt the blows and yet didn't feel them. He had something in his pocket worth all of them.

*

The siege ended two days later.

McLennan realised that his messengers had miscarried. No help was coming. He sensed, with a warrior's instinct, that McInnes was puffed up with assurance of success and might be off his guard. He also knew that he couldn't expect his fighting men to wait much longer.

Leaving the protection of the castle, across the drawbridge, was deadly dangerous. But there was nothing else for it: they must meet the enemy in the open.

That night Bruce McLennan mustered his hungry fighters in the ward, lit dimly by a few torches, and passed the word quietly. 'No help is coming. We canna wait longer.' They knew it. They knew the risks, but they were ready and primed for action. McLennan looked all around them. Their faces, hollow-eyed in the torchlight, gazed back at him like hunting dogs straining at their leashes. A certain belated pride in them stirred him. He had good people.

McLennan gave them their marching orders and then said in a piercing undertone, 'The man who brings me McInnes alive shall be my heir.'

*

The silence of dawn was broken by the thunderous rattle of chains as the drawbridge was swiftly lowered and the great spiked portcullis raised. McLennan's force burst through the narrow gateway like water out of the neck of a bottle, and clattered across the bridge and down the ramp. Roaring like lions, they spread out and rushed down the hill like the hounds of hell, falling upon the soldiers of McInnes just as their lookouts were waking them with shouts of alarm. There was no time to do anything but jump to their feet and snatch up their weapons before McLennan's furious horde was upon them.

Though fewer in number and hungry, the attackers' outrage gave them strength. Every taunt, every sneering act of cruelty and arrogance, had to be repaid. McLennan's men drove McInnes's back and back till they reached the edge of the village. Against the palisade was a long rampart of earth. Many were driven up this in hand-to-hand swordfights, and shoved over the edge, or even impaled on the sharp spikes at the top of the wooden palings. Those who got through the gates were pursued, some driven off their feet and rolling backwards down the hill until spears or swords pinioned them to the ground. All through the half-ruined village there were bloody skirmishes.

And now the furious villagers, immured for days in the village hall, burst out and joined in the fray. They found pitchforks and scythes and stones and wooden clubs and laid about them with all their pent-up strength. The women who had had to submit to the enemy's brutality were the fiercest. Five or six would attack one man and hack and beat him to the ground, screaming dementedly. McInnes's men were prepared to face anything but the women, who rushed after them in packs like hunting wolves, waving carving knives and bunches of flaming straw. Many men ran on to their enemy's pikes as they fled, looking not where they were going but wildly back over their shoulders.

McLennan had led his men out of the castle, but soon was struggling like them in the turmoil of battle. He had one main objective – the capture of McInnes. But in the confusion he missed him. McInnes, unseated, wounded in three places and streaming blood, managed to remount his terrified horse and lead a disorderly rout, abandoning their civilian prisoners and their wounded, who didn't survive long to endure their injuries.

But the fleeing men and their leader did not get far.

Those of McLennan's party who had fled the field six days before had their own scores to settle. They were waiting in ambush in the wooded and craggy hinterland between the two castles, and as the routed men straggled back to McInnes's land, they had rough entertainment. Very few reached their homes.

As for Archibald McInnes — a young man whose house had been burned and his mother murdered — he saw his chance, as McLennan had done years before when he saved the King's life. He knocked the weakened enemy leader from the saddle with his stave, took him prisoner, and marched him back to the castle. He hadn't heard the proclamation, of course, and had no idea that he was destined to be the next laird. But he knew it that night, when McLennan, as good as his word, proclaimed him his heir in front of the castle gate when the struggle was over.

*

And while the battle raged, two children fought their own battle in a dark, silent place, out of earshot of the roars and curses and screams and clashes of the fighting beyond the castle walls.

Peony lay on the floor of the dungeon with her head in

Fin's lap. He held her tenderly and with everything that was in him, his will and his voice and his hands, urged her to live. He dared not leave her to get help; he dared not try to move her. With strips torn from his shirt, he had tied up the wound she had given herself, and successfully staunched the blood. Just the same, his instinct told him he had stolen the key and come to rescue her too late.

Peony was drifting.

Fin had snatched a torch as he ran down to open her prison door, so there was light again, wonderful, magical light, and this had changed everything for her. This, and Fin, who was with her, holding her hand. But he was pulling her back from where she so much wanted to go.

She smiled up at him. 'I must visit my garden,' she whispered.

He cried, 'No, Wee Eyes, no! Don't go to any garden, stay here with me, please stay here with me!' He clung to her as if to stop her running away.

But Peony just smiled and closed her eyes. She was already in her garden. All was changed there. The paths were clear of leaves. Through shafts of sunlight, a fine misty rain was falling like a silver veil, making the pebble-patterns gleam. A rainbow curved over her pavilion, which was once again glossy and beautiful, with exquisite, mysterious music coming from it. And there was Fin, sitting on her verandah in one of the carved chairs under a scrolled hanging, painted with beautiful sprays of her name-flower.

'This is gie good!' he exclaimed approvingly. 'I like your pond! Ye've some grand fishies in there!' Peony glanced over the rail of her bridge and saw that the pond was clear of weed and that red and white carp, large and small, were once again swimming lazily among the lily pads, which shone bright as emeralds in the mixture of sunshine and soft rain.

She felt her heart soar. Her garden had forgiven her! It had healed itself! She dared to look up at the roof-corners.

They were there – her dragons were back! And this time they didn't turn their heads. She felt as if she smiled with all of herself. She lifted her hand and waved to them. They twitched their ears and unrolled their long tongues out of their mouths and nodded their big, ugly-beautiful heads in greeting.

'Fin, Fin!' she called excitedly. 'Come! See my friends!'

And Fin, his figure a misty blur, crossed the crooked bridge and stood at her side. 'They're fine and grand,' he said, his voice full of admiration. 'I never saw such a garden, never. Ye've made the most loveliest garden there is, Mudan.' He put his arm round her and kissed her cheek.

She turned to him with a glad look. But now his voice came again, as if from a distant place, and there was pain in it. 'I'll come back for ye, I promise! I promise!' And she echoed his words like a sigh. 'I'll come back, I promise.' And he seemed to lose solidity and then to vanish.

But though she couldn't see him any more, still he had said her name — her real name! She need not repeat '*Wo shi mudan*' to herself or fight to hold fast to who she was, because now someone who loved her had confirmed her reality. But quite slowly, she found that who she was no longer mattered.

She was just part of her garden.

Chapter Fourteen

McLennan was beside himself with triumph. He had him! He had his enemy at last in his power! His old foe slumped, bound hand and foot, in a wooden chair, grey-faced from defeat and fear as well as loss of blood. McLennan, standing over him, said just three words.

'Now ye'll pay.'

He turned on his heel. But as he reached the door, McInnes's voice halted him.

'What will I pay for? Raiders who exceeded their orders?'

McLennan whirled to face him. 'Ye admit ye sent those barbarous brutes against me!'

'Aye, I sent them, but not to slaughter your children. I sent them to pay ye back for the murder of my sister's son. I could ha' done no less, with her on my neck day and night crying for satisfaction.'

'Murder ye call it? When he and the henchmen you sent with him were trying to drive my people off my land so you could claim it?'

McInnes slumped further into his chair and turned his head aside. McLennan could see now that he was old, and that the old quarrels were nothing to him but a burdensome memory that couldn't be shaken off.

'Och, what's the use of bandying words about it ten years on?'

Balked of the verbal battle he now wanted, McLennan spat at the man. 'Ye cowardly blackguard!' he shouted.

McInnes straightened himself as well as he could.

'Coward, am I? And what are you? When your wife was first lost to ye and brought to me, I posted every guard I had, thinking ye'd be riding against me within hours, alone if necessary – but ye never came. Why not? Did ye no' want her, thinking that she was now spoilt goods?'

McLennan stood before him, shocked and stunned. How dared the man, helpless as he was, speak thus! But he himself had uttered the word 'coward' first.

'I didna come,' he returned in a deathly quiet voice,

Chapter Fourteen

'because for two months after ye had my wee'uns butchered and stole my wife from me, I was out of my senses. Those attending on me had to tie me down and drug me with whiskey to control my raving. By the time I came to myself, word was brought to me that my wife—' He stopped, clenching his teeth.

'Aye,' said McInnes, now equally hushed. 'Aye. If I weren't afraid ye'd think I was trying to pacify ye, I'd tell ye that I was sorry for her death. I never purposed it. I never purposed the deaths of your children.'

'Be wary, ye liar!' barked McLennan. 'I have means to do worse than imprison ye—'

'Your wife,' McInnes went on wearily, 'whom my men brought back to me expecting reward – I didna mean to keep her – I was going to send her back to ye but—'

McLennan stood perfectly still.

'She was stalwart for ye. She wouldna take food or drink, and then she sickened of low fever and died.'

'Of low fever? Liar! She died of shame!'

'No, McLennan. I swear to ye. Not that. She suffered no more shame than confinement and some taunts from my sister.'

'Either way, ye killed her. *Ye killed all that was best of me and in me.*

And now I have ye and the price is to be paid.'

And the image of his dungeon rose to his mind, a dark, cruel image. For this he had had it made and now it would fulfil its purpose! He would lock this enemy in and never—

In the very act of walking from the room, McLennan stopped cold.

He remembered with a shock like a lightning strike who was there already.

He was stunned by the realisation. Six days she had been down there, without food or water, alone in the dark! His hard heart trembled, and his hand flew to his belt. But the key! The key was gone.

It took him ten full seconds to realise that the stable-boy had stolen it, that night he had tried to stab him. That meant—

The relief was what unmanned him. Pure, hot, naked relief. That was three days ago! He would have gone down there, that boy, opened that great door, and let her out. It was all right. She was alive, she was safe, the boy would have saved her.

A prayer – the first genuine prayer to have issued from him in years – left his dry lips.

'Thank God! Thank God!'

But was it certain? What if the key had slipped his belt some other way? What if – what if she were still there?

He ran from the room and down the dungeon steps, his snatched-up torch trailing smoke. He had not felt fear all the time the enemy was at his gates. Now he was afraid – mortally afraid of what he would find.

As the torchlight touched the door, he saw it was open and the key in the lock. His hopes rocketed upwards. Yes, it was as he'd thought! She'd been freed! What he felt, he couldn't disguise from himself – it was pure happiness. Again he cried out a prayer of gratitude, 'Blessed Christ, be praised—'

But as he entered the dungeon and swept the torch about, letting the light flicker on the stone walls, the iron rings, the chains, his prayer died. For there she was, a little, crumpled shape, lying on the floor in the farthest corner.

He rushed towards her, and fell on his knees at her side. As he had once before, he put his hand on her throat to feel for her pulse. He started back, his fingers wet, horror running over his skin. He saw the sharp stone near her hand.

After a long moment of paralysis, he stood up slowly. His legs were unsteady. He kept staring down at her. Then he began to shout, a high note of desperation like a shrill trumpet blast ringing round the cold walls.

'A body can live eight days without food! But ye couldna wait! Why did ye believe me? Ye should ha' known! Ye should ha' known I didna mean it!'

Something strange was happening to his eyes. The torchlight was glistening and he couldn't see properly. He dropped the torch on the stones and put his face in both his hands. His big shoulders heaved and he stood there for what might have been minutes or hours, lost to all sense of himself, feeling only the most agonising regret. Then he picked up the smouldering torch and turned away. He couldn't bear to stay there.

But as he was leaving, the torchlight showed him something scratched on the wall. It was the writing of Chi-na.

He stopped and stared at it, his breath billowing out in clouds like a terrified stag cornered in a frozen field. He hadn't seen such writing for years. But he understood what was written as well as if the words were being spoken in his ears.

'I am with you till you die.'

He stood there, bereft, stunned, and afraid to the marrow

of his bones. Then he turned and fled, stopping only to heave the door shut. But the key would not budge, and he left it in the lock.

*

McLennan couldn't chain his enemy in the dungeon. He couldn't even think about the dungeon. Instead, he had him shut into an upper room in one of the castle turrets. But he ordered bread and water to be given him. How was it he was feeding his enemy when he had let the girl starve?

But decisions, work and responsibilities pressed in on him too heavily to allow much time for reflections. Many of his tenants were dead or hurt. Farmhouses and crops had been destroyed. The men who had been left outside the castle at the time of the siege were very angry. It was rumoured that some had deserted him and fled to other landowners, carrying news of what had happened, blackening his name. Even McLennan's own servants were angry because he had left so many families at the enemy's mercy. After years of caring nothing for what anyone thought of him, suddenly he was vulnerable. He felt they were against him and no longer wanted to serve him. After their brave fight for him, remorse awakened and smote him.

It wasn't in his nature to show that he was sorry. But he

gave the survivors gold to rebuild their farms and buy more animals. He buried the dead with honour, and paid the widows and orphans compensation. Then his strict duty was done. The sullen, angry looks from his household, the rumors of defection, stopped. But he had no satisfaction from it.

Once he might have eased his mind by going to gloat over his captive, to accuse him and torment him. He couldn't, and he didn't understand why he couldn't. McInnes was at last his prisoner, but every time the word 'prisoner' crossed his thoughts, McLennan twisted his mind away.

When one day news was brought to him that McInnes had died of his wounds, he felt not the smallest quiver of gladness. 'Bury him,' was all he said. 'No marker. Let his name be forgotten.' And a strange premonition came to him. *I too wullna have a stone on my grave.*

The death of his old enemy did nothing to restore his peace. At night he slept badly. He had terrible dreams. Over and over again, the same one – the child in chains. He heard chains rattling in his sleep. When he woke suddenly, he thought he could still hear them. He lay on his bed, staring upward into the dark, and tears, such as he had not shed since the deaths of his own children, rolled down the sides of his face and soaked his silken sheets. The red of them made him feel as if he slept in a pool of blood.

'I didna chain her! At least I didna chain her! Why do I hear chains?' he muttered.

Sometimes he saw her face, pale and bloodless, and sometimes he felt her cold little hands touching him. He would reach for them before he could stop himself, the impulse to rub and warm them back to life was so strong. Sometimes he heard clicking sounds, like bones knocking and scraping each other. Once he dreamed he went down to the dungeon and opened the door, and there was a little skeleton, standing upright. Peony's slanted eyes were peering at him through the sockets in the skull. In his dream he found he wanted to embrace it – to clasp all that was left of her in his arms. But when he laid hands on the skeleton, it fell to the floor in a heap of bones.

He feared he was going mad. And yet he almost welcomed it, because madness would be an escape from his sorrow, his bewilderment. 'She was a slave! A witch!' he tried to tell himself. But he knew now she had been neither, that she had been his little one, his dear one, the child fate had sent him as a gift to comfort his heart which had been too hard to feel the love for her that had grown there all unrecognised.

Only now when it was too late did he know it.

His body seemed to shrink. He no longer walked tall, with his plaid lifting on the breeze behind him. His beard grew wild and untrimmed; he wouldn't let anyone touch him. His arms hung at his sides. His face was pale and drawn, his eyes were unfocussed.

'He's no' the man he was,' muttered his servants.

'It's the wee witch,' the goblin-cook whispered. 'Witches dunna die quiet and they dunna lie quiet. She's haunting him.'

Some of the women said they'd seen her. Fin, deep in grief, heard them.

'Wee Eyes! Come to me! Haunt me, I dunna mind, so ye'll come!' he whispered in the night.

His parents were safe, and neither of the other boys had been killed in the battle – they had fought bravely, and brought honour on the family that McLennan now rewarded. They went back to their burnt-out farmhouse and rebuilt it with their own labour and McLennan's money. They cursed him, but what else could they do? Many of their neighbours were doing the same. Life had to go on.

Janet grew big and the family began to look ahead to the birth of the new baby, and to be a little happy again. Fin alone didn't join in. He could only think of Wee Eyes, and of avenging her. He watched McLennan and, when he could, followed him about like his shadow. He always knew where he was.

*

One day, after yet another terrible night of dreams and fantasies, McLennan could stand it no longer.

'I'll away down there and take her out and bury her,' he thought. 'That'll be the end of it. It's because I didna give her decent burial that she wullna let me be.'

He took a torch and went down the steps to the dungeon. His knees were knocking and the torch shook in his hand, casting demonic shadows on the stone walls. The key was where he had left it, in the lock. He pulled the door open. He walked slowly to the corner where he'd last seen Peony.

She was gone.

All trace of her was gone. Even the bloodstain. Everything. Except the characters scratched on the wall.

'I am with you till you die.'

McLennan felt his head swim. He hadn't eaten or slept properly for weeks. Now he felt himself falling. He fell just where Peony had lain, and lay there in a dead faint.

Some time later, he woke up. It was a screeching sound that roused him. His torch had gone out – he was in darkness. But he knew that sound. It was the key turning in the lock of the dungeon door.

He jumped to his feet and threw himself against it. He cried out, as she had cried, 'Och, dunna! Dunna! Dunna!' He didn't hear the sound of feet climbing the steps. And of course he never heard the distant splash of the key falling into the river.

But still, his death was not as difficult as perhaps he deserved. The scratched words on the dungeon wall came true another way. For McLennan the darkness of his dungeon was not empty, and although he languished there for many, many days, and lost his mind completely, in the end he did not die alone.

Epilogue

结尾

Fin's little sister was born a few months after the laird of the castle disappeared.

She was a bonny child, with her father's reddish hair but with curiously dark eyes, even from her birth. She brought a feeling of new life and happiness to the family, who all rejoiced in their first girl-child. They called her by a flower name, Heather, and they all doted on her. Fin carried her about with him whenever he could. The first time she looked up at him in a 'seeing' way, and smiled, showing she recognised him, Fin knew that he was going to love her more than anyone.

He told her fairy stories. The Little People he told about had long black hair, golden skins, and beautiful slanting eyes.

He called them the Wee-Eyed Ones.

The years passed.

When Heather was old enough, one day Fin took her by the hand and led her to a secret place in a copse of trees. There was a little grave there. It didn't have a cross. It had a rowan tree growing from it instead.

'That's my Wee Eyes, down there,' Fin said. 'I promised her, when she died, that I'd come back for her. And two nights after the siege ended, I crept back down there and brought her out. It was sooty-dark and I dared not carry a light, but I found her by touch, and brought her up the steps, crept out by the postern gate and carried her all the way back home here in the dark. And I buried her. She wasna a Christian so I had to make up some prayers, specially for her. I did right by her. And now we've a new laird who is better than the old one. And I've got you, and you're going to have a good life. I'll see to it, and that's a promise I'll keep, like I kept mine to her.'

And the little girl turned her strange dark eyes up at him, full of trust, and nodded as if she knew it all already.